"Allow me to introduce myself. I'm the Durango Kid," said the 808 rider. "That's because I got my first man in Durango when I was a kid. I'm older and one hell of a lot meaner now. But I'll tell you what I'm going to do for you, squash hat. I'm going to count to ten. Then, if you're still here, or if I see you, later, anywhere in this town, I mean to lay you low. So study on it afore I get to ten."

Then he started counting, slow, as everyone else shut up to see what was going to happen next.

Taylor didn't cotton much to crawfishing. On the other hand . . .

THE BUNTLINE SPECIAL

Lou Cameron

FAWCETT GOLD MEDAL • NEW YORK

A Fawcett Gold Medal Book
Published by Ballantine Books
Copyright © 1988 by Lou Cameron

Library of Congress Catalog Card Number: 88-91168

ISBN 0-449-13357-5

Manufactured in the United States of America

First Edition: November 1988

THE BUNTLINE SPECIAL

Matt Taylor doubted the man he was hunting had the sand in his craw for a serious showdown. So he rode into the trail town of Freewater at sundown, sedate, with his Winchester in its saddle boot and just five safe rounds in the wheel of his Colt .44–40.

He'd passed through Freewater before, herding cows for that larcenous cuss, Grat Lewis. So he knew the Prairie Dog Saloon gave the best value in town, and he hoped the cheap bastard he was after might remember that.

Taylor reined in when he got to the Prairie Dog. He could see by the ponies already tethered out front that word had gotten out about every third drink being on the house. He dismounted to find just enough room at one end of the hitching rail to tether his own paint gelding. Then he adjusted his cross-draw rig for walking instead of riding and mounted the plank steps to part the bat wings of the establishment. The light inside would have have been just a mite tricky without the blue haze of tobacco smoke that veiled the features of the gents toward the rear of the cavernous taproom. So Taylor stayed put, a thin, bitter smile on his lips as he swept the crowd with slightly

1

narrowed eyes. His heart was pure. He was only after one
particular son of a bitch. So he was not at all aware of the
disturbing picture he made, looming there in the doorway.

Matt Taylor thought of himself as a friendly cuss, and he
was, most of the time. As a top hand he spent more on his
spurred black Justins and pancaked black Stetson than the
practical denim duds that covered the rest of him. His six-
gun was, to him, just a tool of his trade. He wore it cross-
draw in a plain black rig because he could get at it easier,
whether mounted or afoot. At the moment he was trail-
dusty and could have used a shave. But he wasn't trying to
look tough. He just did.

Failing to spot the man he was hunting, Taylor strode
over to the bar, found a gap near one end, and ordered a
needled beer. As the barkeep served Taylor, he observed
mildly, "I can see you're a stranger here, sir. It's none of my
business, of course, but our town law, Big Bill Burton,
takes a dim view of displaying such hardware on one's hip
as you seem to fancy."

Taylor placed a quarter on the mahogany beside his beer
schooner as he replied, in as friendly a tone, "Do tell? I'd
have never suspicioned you had a gun ordinance in these
parts, judging from the guns half the gents in here seem to
be wearing."

The barkeep leaned closer, confidentially, and explained,
"The 808 herd just come up from the Indian Nation. Them
riders you see wearing Texan hats and mayhaps a few guns
don't figure to be in town all that long, see?"

Taylor sipped some suds, put the schooner down again,
and confided, "I don't mean to spend much time here
myself. I am searching for Grat Lewis, the trail boss of the
consolidated market herd you may recall passing through
here just a week or more back."

The barkeep shrugged and said. "We get lots of herds
passing through this time of the year. That's why we built

this town on the Ogallala Trail to begin with. You say this pal you're looking for was your trail boss?"

Taylor frowned and replied, "I'd hardly call him a pal. When we got the herd up to the Ogallala stockyards he sort of forgot to pay us off. He owes me a dollar and a half a day for more otherwise unrewarding days on the trail than I like to study on. Some of the others he cheated think he lit out by rail with our back wages. But I noticed his fine Morgan pony was missing as well. So it's my personal persuasion he's riding back to Texas in solitary splendor, faster than I thought if he's already made it past here."

The barkeep whistled mournsome and said, "No offense, but I'm sort of glad. We just mopped the floor and spread fresh sawdust. I'd feel safer stealing a man's woman than day wages he *rode herd* for!"

Taylor shrugged and said, "Old Grat never struck me as a man with the brains of a gnat. I'll just have me a look-see around your fair city, and if he ain't here, I'll just have to look for him farther down the trail."

Taylor meant that and would have just finished his beer and been on his way had not four more 808 riders come busting in through the bat wings with a rebel yell, and had not one of them pushed him rudely and told him, "You'd best git, cowboy. There ain't room at this here bar for the 808 and anyone else."

Taylor didn't move. He said, "I'll be proud to leave as soon as I finish these suds I paid for. Meanwhile, you'd best keep your hands to yourself, lest you draw back a stump."

The rougher-looking rider who'd already pushed him more often than Taylor admired being pushed stared at him in wonder for a pregnant eight or ten seconds. Then he announced joyously, "Hey boys, this pilgrim talks! Mean as hell, too! How come you talk so mean, little darling?"

The barkeep paled and murmured, "Take it easy, Mule. The man just said he was leaving soon."

But Mule, as he was so aptly called, growled, "Stay out of my ear lest I swat you, barfly. This skinny rascal with his pretty hat crushed north range just raised his girlish voice to me. So now we're fixing to dance the Hooley-Ann. Ain't that right, little darling?"

Taylor shrugged and replied, "If you say so." But then another 808 rider hauled Mule out of the way to take his place, sticking out his chest at Taylor as he announced softly, "Mule ain't good as me with a gun, and I see you're armed. So allow me to introduce myself. I am best knowed as the Durango Kid. That's because I got my first man in Durango when I was a kid. I'm older and one hell of a lot meaner now. But I'll tell you what I'm going to do for you, squash hat. I'm going to count to ten. Then, if you're still here, or if I see you later anywhere in this town, I mean to lay you low. So study on it afore I get to ten."

Then he started counting, slow, as everyone else shut up to see what was going to happen next.

Taylor didn't cotton much to crawfishing. On the other hand, he only had five rounds to work with, and there were more than two dozen gents in the joint with their hats creased the same way. He knew that they expected him to back down. He knew the so-called Durango Kid would back down if the situation were reversed, and he knew that whether they laughed at him or not, he'd never see the silly bastards again, and more important, he knew he'd still be alive.

So he might have backed down. He was considering it, at least, by the time the Durango Kid got to "Six!" But then the bat wings crashed open to admit a mighty big man with a mighty big gun. The Durango Kid stopped counting as the burly giant's overgrown six-gun roared at the pressed-tin ceiling for attention and the one and original Big Bill Burton thundered, "Freeze! Ever' damn one of you! What's going on in here, Sean?"

The barkeep sighed and said, "Damn it, Marshal, I wish you'd stop perforating my poor ceiling like that. The boys here was just having a friendly argument."

Big Bill stared soberly down at everyone from his considerable height. He stood at least seven foot one on his high heels, and as if that weren't scary enough, his gun-muzzle-gray eyes stared coldly out of a face that seemed carved from granite as he waved the sixteen-inch barrel of his .45 about as if he thought he was a concert master waving a baton for pianissimo.

He got it. In the hushed silence Big Bill's disgusted growl carried to every corner of the saloon as he observed, "I thought I told you 808 riders you could keep your sidearms as long as you *behaved* yourselves here in Freewater. Is this any way to repay my sweet and understanding nature? Goddamn your mother's eyes!"

The Durango Kid stared hard at Matt Taylor as he tried, "This other cuss started it, Marshal. He called poor old Mule, who ain't as noted a gun-slick as me. You can see for yourself the cuss has a gun on his hip as well as a chip on his shoulder. What was we supposed to do, let him rawhide us as if we was sissies?"

Another Texan called out from the safety of the rear of the pack, "Whoo-hee-haw! The Alamo and the 808!"

Big Bill Burton silenced him with a wave of his freak gun and told the Durango Kid, "I saw what you was doing just in time, you lucky cuss. If two on one is dago fun, what would you call at least two dozen on one, heroic?"

Mule grinned and said, "Aw, he'd have backed down, Marshal."

But the giant in the doorway stared soberly at Taylor to decide. "Maybe. You'd best come along with me, young fellow."

"On what charge?" asked Taylor mildly. Then he found himself staring down the long barrel of the marshal's .45.

The big man could sure swing that cannon to cover lots of territory. So when Big Bill repeated, "I said to come with me," Taylor picked up his change, left his beer right where it was, and went with him.

Outside, Big Bill said soberly, "When I was your age I paid more heed to my elders. That's no doubt how I got to be my age. Would you have gone for broke or crawfished back there, had not I spotted what was going on in time to put a stop to it?"

Taylor replied truthfully, "I don't know. I didn't much like either ending to the story. Where are you taking me, to the town lockup?"

Big Bill chuckled and replied, "Yep, but not to lock you up. I admire a man with hair on his chest, as long as he don't overdo it. I'm a peace officer. My job is to keep the peace here in this town. I feel that'll be a lot easier if only I can keep you and the 808 apart till they ride on, come sunrise. So I got almost a full bottle of Kentucky mash in my desk drawer, and my office will be the safest place in town for you to drink until that passel of pesky Texicans rides on. What do they call you, old son?"

Taylor identified himself and added, "I used to be from Texas, too. Amarillo County, in the Panhandle. Our spread got froze off in the big blue norther of eighty-seven. So I've been working for other outfits since."

Big Bill answered, "Do tell? How come you wear your hat the north-range style, then?"

Taylor shrugged and said, "Same reason north-range riders crush their hats. To keep it from blowing off. The winds sure blow, north of the Arkansas Divide."

By this time they'd made it to the marshal's office. Big Bill ushered Taylor into the modest office out front of the cell block and waved him to a bentwood chair as he, in turn, sat down behind a paper-cluttered desk and slid open a drawer to produce the promised bourbon, along with two coffee mugs. As he poured drinks indeed, Big Bill placed his awkwardly long-barreled gun atop the papers on the desk. Taylor had been wondering how one might holster such a weapon. As Big Bill handed Taylor one of the mugs, he nodded and said, "My Buntline Special's sort of clumsy to draw. But it makes up for it once it's in my hand."

Taylor took a cautious sip, grimaced, and said, "I noticed. How come you call it a Buntline anything? No offense, but from here it looks like a product of Colt Arms."

Big Bill leaned back in his more comfortable chair, enjoyed a good slug of bourbon, and explained, "It *was* made by Colt, as a special order. Ned Buntline had just six of 'em made up to his own design. You've heard of Ned Buntline, of course?"

Taylor took another sip—the second one wasn't as painful—before he said cautiously, "I've heard the name. Ain't he a penny-dreadful writer, back east, who makes up stories about cowboys and Indians?"

Big Bill sighed and told him, "*Was,* son, past tense. For, alas, old Ned's no longer with us. He went to the Happy Hunting Ground in eighty-seven, just about the time your folk was getting froze off, as a matter of fact."

Taylor stared at the gun on the desk between them as he asked, "How come a gent who only *writ* about cowboys and Indians needed such a heap of special six-guns?"

To which his older mentor sadly replied, "As presents, son. He ordered them guns made special so he could present 'em to western heroes he admired, in honor of the way they'd helped to win the West, see?"

Taylor still looked uncertain. So Big Bill explained, "He come out to Dodge in the year of our Lord 1876 and helt a special ceremony at the Long Branch for us."

"Us?" asked Taylor. So Big Bill nodded modestly and explained, "There was Charly Bassett, Neal Brown, Wyatt

Earp, Bat Masterson, Bill Tilghman, and me, of course. At that time the six of us was regarded as the foremost lawmen west of the Big Muddy. So we each got the same special guns from Ned Buntline, and that's how come they're called Buntline Specials."

He reached out with his free hand to run his fingertips gently over the hardwood grips of the long-barreled monster as he added, "You'll never see the likes of this old beauty made again, now that old Ned is dead. But ain't she something? Sixteen-inch barrel, and do you want, you can fit her with a special stock and use her as a rifle. A carbine, leastways. I don't know what ever become of that detaching stock as come in the box Ned presented to me in the Long Branch. I know I never left it there, drunk as we all got that evening. I might have left it ahint when I had to leave Johnson County so sudden."

Taylor whistled softly and asked, "Good grief, were you mixed up in the Johnson County War, Big Bill?"

The older man sighed wistfully and admitted, "Not on the side that won, in the end. But I got out in time, alive, which is the point I was trying to make about you and the 808 outfit, old son. There's times to stand your ground and there's times when even us heroes have to call it too big a boo. You wasn't looking for no one-sided war with the 808 in the first place, was you?"

Taylor shook his head and brought Big Bill up-to-date on his personal feud with Grat Lewis while they both sipped at their mugs. By the time he'd run out of mean things to call Lewis, his mug was about empty. So Big Bill leaned forward to refill it before he settled back to growl, "A man who'd steal back pay his hands had coming would no doubt pimp for his mother if his sister was too ugly. This ain't the first time I've heard about a trail boss named Lewis. I think he done the same thing to another bunch a year or so back.

What are your intentions toward the cuss, once you track him down, ah, Matt?"

Taylor shrugged and said, "You have to eat the apple one bite at a time. So far I ain't seen hide nor hair of him since he told us to meet him later, up Nebraska way. I don't expect to have to gun him. He's more a sneak thief than an armed robber. So it's my sincere hope he'll fork over what he owes me without a fight, if only I can corner him long enough to ask, sort of firm."

Big Bill nodded, inhaled some more bourbon, then said sagely, "Meanwhile you have to be mighty low on pocket jingle, and just suppose you never catch up with him?"

Taylor grimaced and said, "I'll wind up even poorer, I reckon. As it is, I'm down to where I can't afford to leave change on the bar."

Big Bill nodded and said, "I noticed. I figured you had to be broke or brave as well as cheap. What would you say to a job as pays ten dollars a week, if someone was to offer it to you?"

Taylor raised an eyebrow and aid, "I'd say it was about as much as I could hope to make herding cows. What's the catch?"

Big Bill said, "No catch. Easy work, nine days outten ten. I need a senior deputy, Matt. The boys I got are good enough for them nine days in ten, but to tell the truth, they ain't worth sheep-dip on that tenth day, when the going gets rougher."

He took another sip, sighed, and went on, "It's sure tedious to find yourself trying to keep the peace all alone, when your backup backs down on you. You don't strike me as a back-down gent, Matt. So how about it? Do you want the job?"

Taylor laughed incredulously and replied, "You can't be serious! I'm a cowhand, not a peace officer. I've had no training in such matters."

The older man shrugged and asked, "Who has? Half the lawmen of today was cow thieves in their misspent youth. That's what makes 'em so good at catching cow thieves. You know how to ride. You know how to handle a gun, and you just this evening proved you had some backbone. That's all I need in a deputy. I can tell you if there's anything else I want you to know. You'll find that, like I said, most of the time there's nothing much to do in a town this size, where most of the folk are calm and reasonsome."

Taylor thought before he said, "I dunno, Big Bill; your offer is sure flattering, and Lord knows I could use the money. But to tell the truth, I'd feel like a fool wearing a badge. I wouldn't know how to talk to folk as a deputy marshal."

Big Bill shrugged and said, "You talk to them about the same as always, unless they're doing something they hadn't ought to. Then you just tell 'em to cut it out, and most of the time, they do."

Taylor raised his mug to his lips to give himself time to think. Big Bill misread the gesture, or perhaps he didn't, and, in any case, asked, "What if I could sweeten the pot for you a mite?"

Taylor asked what he had in mind. Big Bill said, "I just can't offer you more money, to start. Raises are up to the infernal city council. But what if I could tell you where the rascal who owes you all that money could be found?"

Taylor gasped and asked, "You *know* where Grat Lewis can be found? No bull?"

Big Bill nodded and explained, "It's my job to know what's going on in my jurisdiction. As a peace officer, I confess I felt things might be more peaceable around here if I just let the son of a bitch ride on. But since I can see you just have your heart set on catching up with him, and since you've assured me you ain't out to kill him unless you have to, I may give him to you, on two conditions, hear?"

"Name them," said Taylor, grim-lipped.

So Big Bill said, "My first condition is that you let me deputize you afore you start after him. My second condition is that you report back here for duty, bright-eyed and bushy-tailed, once you settle accounts with the trail boss who cheated you. Agreed?"

"I dunno. How far are we talking about me trailing him?"

"He's here in town. That's all you get until I badge you."

Taylor grinned wolfishly and said, "Well, hell, pin the fool badge on me and let me *at* the son of a bitch!"

The evening was still young, but Grat Lewis wasn't. A hard day's ride, a hot meal, and the lukewarm pleasures to be found in the arms of a soiled dove had conspired to send him to bed early. So he was enjoying the sleep of the unjust in Freewater Fannie's house of ill repute when Matt Taylor woke him up, sort of rudely, by pouring the contents of a handy chamber pot all over him.

The befuddled victim of this wet awakening rolled off the bed in his soggy red flannel union suit, spitting crud and curses as he groped blindly for the gun belt he'd draped over the back of a bedside chair. His gun wasn't there. Then Taylor kicked him, chair and all, into a far corner before he announced laconically, "I got your gun and the gal out of harm's way afore I felt ready to wake you up. Are you awake, you thieving son of a bitch?"

The larcenous trail boss sat up amid the splintered remains of the chair as he wiped his face on a red flannel sleeve and whined, "I've a good mind to have the law on you for treating me so uncivilized. Is this your notion of a Halloween prank, damn it? If it is, you're nigh a full month early."

Then Taylor struck a match to light the wall lamp, and Lewis added warily, "Oh. Howdy, Matt. I hope you got the check I left for you with the stockyard paymaster when I was called home on urgent business."

Taylor stared down at him in disgusted silence until he saw improvised baptism already seemed to be saving some tedious conversation, if not Grat's soul. He chucked and asked, "Do you always wear your money belt under your union suit like that?" To which the soggy Lewis could only reply, with a sad little shrug, "I got to wear it somewheres, don't I? How come we have to keep talking finances, Matt? I just told you I left any money I might have owed to you with that gent up Nebraska-way. He assured me he'd see you and the rest of the boys got what was due you all."

Taylor grimaced and said, "Now I'll tell one. At the current price of beef on the hoof, a scrub cow one can buy in Texas for five or six bucks can be sold in Nebraska for fifty or sixty. So you contracted to drive a herd of the same up to Ogallala. Then, since you couldn't hardly drive such a herd all by yourself, you hired me and the other boys to help you. We did, and we only lost four head, in a six-hundred-mile drive that had us eating dust for a full month. We wouldn't have lost *any* if you'd paid heed to my warning against trying to ford the Arkansas in that infernal thunderstorm. But let's say it was our fault just the same. You still owe each and every one of us close to forty bucks in wages after you deduct top dollar, say, two hundred, for the stock we lost on you."

The older as well as wetter man sat up straighter as he shook his head and protested, "You got me all wrong, Matt. Docking you boys for them drowned cows never crossed my mind. Like I said, I left checks for each and every one of you as I was leaving for home, unexpected, on pathetical family matters. My poor sister's eldest boy needs this operation to restore his sight and—"

"Sheep-dip," Taylor cut in, adding, "Me and the boys never hired on with you as eye doctors. Aside from which, you told the paymaster in Ogallala it was your sweet little daughter who's took sick of a sudden. Yes, we did talk to him, and no, he didn't say a word about any *dinero* you'd left in his care. He did observe you'd played much the same dirty trick on your hands after an earlier drive, though. He said you was a caution and seemed to find you amusing. I don't. So on your feet, you common thief."

The crooked trail boss slid up the wall to his bare feet. He wiped one gingerly on the edge of the rug and muttered, "That do feel disgusting, even when it's mostly your own. Calm your fool self down and let's settle this like sensible businessmen. I'll just give you your back wages in cash and put a stop on that old check you seem to be so confused about, right?"

"Wrong," said Taylor, ticking the brass badge pinned to his shirtfront with the steel muzzle of his .44-40 as he explained, "You ain't getting off that easy now. I'd have likely had a heap more trouble catching up with you if I hadn't agreed to ride for the law. Now that I have, things ain't just between you and me no more. As a lawman, it's my duty to uphold the law, and embezzlement is a statute felony, even afore you cross state lines with other folk's money."

Lewis tried, "Oh, hell, I just said I'd give you your money, and just to prove my good intent, what say I throw in a hundred-dollar bonus?"

. But Taylor shook his head and insisted, "You're a crook. It's my sworn duty as a deputy marshal of Freewater Township to arrest any crooks I see in or about this township. So haul on your duds and do so sudden, unless you want me to frog-march you to the lockup in your union suit."

He sounded like he meant it, and he had the drop on his man, so Lewis grudgingly got dressed, protesting all the while that Taylor was *loco en la cabeza* and that he meant to sue the whole damned town for false arrest.

Lewis was still bitching, a quarter hour later, when Taylor shoved him in a patent cell, minus his gun rig and money belt, of course. Taylor locked the cell door and strode out to the front office to hang up the key ring and put Grat's arms and cash in the desk drawer for safekeeping. He'd just done so when Big Bill Burton came back from wherever he'd just been to ask, "Well, old son, did you get your money off that rascal at the cathouse?"

Taylor smiled thinly and replied, "I got him and all the money entire. I just locked him up in the back, ah, boss."

Big Bill frowned thoughtfully and asked, "How come? What's the charge you figured we could hold him on?"

Taylor frowned back, even more puzzled, to reply, "What charge, my foot! I told you he run off with a whole damn payroll, and I just now *caught* him with it. Most of it, leastways. I figured you and me ought to count it together afore we notify the boys by wire. I put it in the bottom drawer on the left."

Big Bill moved around his desk to take his seat as he sighed and said, "From now on you'd best check with me afore you go out arresting folk on your own, Matt. Our job is to keep trouble *out* of Freewater, not to *import* none."

He opened the drawer to haul out the heavy money belt and heft it with a whistle as Taylor insisted, "I never asked that crook to hole up here in Freewater. It was his own grand notion, damn it."

Big Bill dropped the evidence back in the drawer and closed it with his boot, saying, "Well, Lord knows the money can't all be rightly his. So maybe we can work something out. We're going to have to do so unofficial, though. Judge Carver would have our poor heads, fried, did we pester him with even a possible felony committed clean out of the state as well as his six-by-six-mile jurisdiction!"

Taylor shook his head as a bull does when there's a hover fly between its horns and protested, "Damn it, Big Bill, you know the man's a crook, I know the man's a crook. The other boys he tried to skin know he's a crook. So why can't your infernal *judge* see he's a crook?"

Big Bill fumbled a cigar from a vest pocket, bit the tip off, and spat it out before he explained, "Judge Carver is stuck with a law degree. He ain't allowed to think sensible as the rest of us about simple justice. You see, old son, there's simple justice, there's Good Book justice, and then there's lawyer justice. Most natural folk and even the Good Book tends to agree on what has to be right and what has to be wrong. But law schools and law books and rascals as take up the law can act contrary as all hell. That's how come one man can wind up in prison for a little fun with a sassy young gal while another man can go free after torturing his mother to death, if he's got the right lawyer."

Big Bill lit his cigar and blew an expansive blue smoke ring at Taylor before adding, "I never went to law school. But I've had a heap of gents I've arrested walk free, smirking at me. So I can tell you what Judge Carver's likely to do if we haul your man afore him. He's going to say Grat Lewis never stole dime one from any resident of Freewater or even Colorado, and then he's going to discharge him for lack of evidence, money and all!"

Taylor set his jaw even firmer to insist, "That's just plain stupid, no offense. I can bear witness he stole from *me*, and I'm a resident of this township now, right?"

Big Bill smiled wryly and said, "Don't push your luck on that point afore folk here in Freewater get used to the notion. Judge Carver would likely ask me to fire you as a pest if you pestered him by picking at that nit. Even I can see you weren't no resident of even this state when your

boss tried to screw you out of your wages in Nebraska.
Lewis ain't a resident of Colorado, any more than you was
when he robbed you in Nebraska. Until or unless he busted
one local law, neither you nor me had any just cause to
arrest him, as far as *statute* law reads, see?"

Taylor scowled and said, "I do now, sort of. But damn it,
it just ain't right, or even sensible, to simply turn the cuss
loose with all that money!"

Big Bill nodded agreeably and said, "I know. So let's
study on it some. Did anyone in town see you bring the gent
in here, as a prisoner under arrest, I mean?"

Taylor thought before he decided, "The gals at the
cathouse must have heard me tell Grat he was under arrest. I
wasn't out to keep it secret."

Big Bill shrugged and said, "Freewater Fannie's gals will
say anything we want 'em to say, should anyone ask. What
about as you brung him from there to here in the gloom of
night?"

Taylor shrugged and said, "It was gloomy, all right. I
don't recall either of us talking to anybody along the way.
Does it matter?"

Big Bill said, "It does," as he got back to his feet. Every
time he loomed like that it took a little getting used to. The
giant lawman hauled the big Buntline Special out from
under his frock coat as he told Taylor, "Bring his gun rig
along with the key ring." So Taylor did as he was told. But
as he caught up with his new boss in front of the cell his old
boss was in, Taylor asked, "Do we have to, boss?"

Big Bill took the key ring from him and said, "We do.
We got to make sure justice is done in these parts," as the
larcenous Lewis rolled off his jail cot to approach the bars
with a wary coyote grin that made Taylor want to just plain
puke. Big Bill unlocked the cell door, telling Lewis, "I'm
Marshal Burton, and I know what you are. You're doubtless
slick enough to see there's an even chance you'd get off if
we pushed this to the expenses of a trial."

Grat licked his lips and said, "I never come here looking for trouble with the law, Marshal."

Big Bill chuckled and said, "I know what occasioned your short stay in Freewater. The gals keep me informed about free-spending strangers, you cheap bastard." Then he waved the crook out of the cell with the batonlike barrel of his freakish Colt and said in a friendlier tone, "We don't want gents like you in this town, Lewis. Where did you say you left your pony?"

Grat gulped and said, "Just down the way, in the livery, and I'll be proud to mount him and ride, if you're really letting me go."

Big Bill looked disgusted and pointed out, "If I didn't want you to go anywheres, I wouldn't have bothered unlocking your door. Give the man his gun, Matt."

Taylor didn't want to, but he did. As Lewis strapped his .38 S&W back on, he seemed to grow at least an inch, and he wasn't half as hangdog as he told Big Bill, "I agreed to pay Matt here the debt he seems to feel I owe him. The rest of the *dinero* in that money belt he took from me is mine, right?"

Big Bill shook his head and poked Lewis with the muzzle of his Buntline Special to herd him toward the front as he growled, "Nope. We're impounding that as evidence, pending full response to some wires Matt here will be sending. Of course, if you ain't in town when and if we find out for sure what a crook you are—"

"I'm going, I'm going!" Grat assured them. But as the three of them crossed the front office to get to the door, their erstwhile prisoner couldn't refrain from grumbling, "This is sure raw, even for a trail town as wide open as this one."

Big Bill said, "Just open the door and git. If you don't like my notions of simple justice, you can always hire a lawyer, you know."

Lewis obviously didn't. But all he said as he opened the

door to step outside was, "Later. *Hasta la vista,* you highway robbers."

Big Bill chuckled indulgently and followed him outside just a few steps before he called out, "Oh, Lewis?" So Grat naturally turned around to see what he wanted. That was when Big Bill swung the long barrel of his Buntline Special up and fired, with the muzzle so close to Grat's chest that it set his shirt on fire.

Lewis landed flat on his back, farther out in the dusty street, his hat in the dust a little farther. As the echoes of Big Bill's single shot faded away down the street, doors and windows were already slamming open in all directions. Taylor discovered he'd stopped breathing, inhaled a bucket of night air, and demanded, "Jesus H. Christ, have you lost your mind entire?"

Big Bill chuckled and replied, "I ain't Jesus H. Christ. I am the law. Let me do the talking and just don't disagree with anything I tell the others, hear?"

"Damn it, Bill, you just cut a man down in cold blood! Is that what you call justice, simple or otherwise?"

"I do. You said he was a dirty thief and I believed you. Lucky for me, I beat him to the draw when he resisted arrest just now. As you know, we only wanted to talk to him about some disturbsome stories we'd heard about him. Lord knows how he might have talked his way out of 'em. But since he refused to talk to us at all, I don't see how he'll ever to able to avoid simple justice *now,* do you?"

By morning the troublesome riders of the 808 outfit had moved on up the trail with their herd. But everyone left in town seemed to want to talk and fuss at once until midafternoon, when the coroner's jury announced its verdict. Matt Taylor was one of the few who found the verdict at all surprising, even though he'd lied through his teeth to back Big Bill's version of his shoot-out with the embezzler on the run. It made Matt feel soiled, and later he felt honor-bound to tell Big Bill right out that he'd have never perjured himself like that for *one* friend alone.

But as Big Bill had pointed out before the coroner's jury met, the boys who'd ridden all the way up the trail with him and the late Grat Lewis, only to be robbed of their just deserts, had no chance of ever getting their back wages unless everyone else could plainly see, by his actions, that Lewis had been up to no good.

Taylor didn't say, but he'd sort of suspected, Grat might not have been the only dishonest man in town until Big Bill backed his notion about wiring the glad tidings to the other old boys cheated by the crooked trail boss. Big Bill even made helpful suggestions as to how one might contact members of a scattered work crew without running up an awesome bill with Western Union. Taylor had to admit he might not have seen how simple it was to just send money orders to each man's home address. Big Bill helped his new deputy count out the cash for each money order, demanded a receipt for each and every one, and explained that even if the rider the money order was made out to took a year getting home, nobody else, even kin, could cash it without his signature.

In the end, after paying out all the back wages from the contents of Grat's money belt, they came out ahead, two ways. The fifty-four dollars and change left over was cash enough to split evenly and not enough to make Taylor feel much more like a dog than he already did. Then they got a wire from the Bureau of Indian Affairs, congratulating Big Bill on finally bringing Grat Lewis to justice and awarding him the twenty-five-hundred bounty the BIA had put on Lewis, dead or alive, for the theft of considerable beef from the Indian Nation a few years back.

Big Bill offered to split that with Taylor as well. Taylor told him not to talk dumb. He felt sick enough about the whole disgusting affair. It made him even sicker to hear Big

Bill brag on his shoot-out with the noted outlaw, modestly enough, it was true, but still a plain-out lie. So as the dinky trail town got calmed down, a day or more later, Taylor unpinned his badge, took it into the office, and dropped it on Big Bill's desk, next to the Buntline Speical.

Big Bill looked up at him to ask mildly, "How come, old son? Ain't we been treating you right?"

Taylor nodded soberly and replied, "You have. The food at that boardinghouse you steered me to is fine, and like you said, they change the bed linens regular and I've yet to see a bug on or off the pillows. But I've done what I come to Freewater to do, and, no offense, I just ain't cut out to be your kind of lawman. So I'd best get it on down the road."

Big Bill sighed and said, "Well, since Lincoln freed all the slaves I can't see my way clear to hold you here against your will, even if you did give your word."

Taylor grimaced and said, "I've thought about that. I'll allow I'd have never caught up with Lewis without your help, if you'll allow you got paid back in spades. Thanks to me bringing him in, you wound up with all that bounty money and got to be even more famous. Don't that make us about even?"

Big Bill shrugged and answsered, "If you say so. I've never put a price on backing a pard or vice versa. As to the fame that just seems to come along with fortune, I got a question for you, old son. Are you jealous because I got all the credit for gunning that worthless polecat?"

Taylor laughed incredulously and said, "Hell's bells, why in thunder should I feel *jealous?* I'd have gunned him myself if he'd really needed gunning."

Big Bill said soberly, "He needed gunning. Mayhaps not for the exact reasons we gave the coroner's jury. But what I done was right, just the same. The man was no damned good. He stole from you and your pals. He even stole from Indians, and you know there was no judge and jury in these

United States as would have put him out of business for good. Habituated crooks like him are too smart to ever commit a hanging offense if they can help it. They just go on and on, making all sorts of folk miserable, till they finally kill somebody or somebody kills them."

He flicked some cigar ash on the bare floor, put the big smoke back in his huge head, and reflected, "Lord knows how many others he'd have crooked, hurt, or even killed if I hadn't done what has to be done with his unseemly kind."

Taylor shrugged and said, "I backed you up at that hearing. I ain't even saying you was in the wrong now. All I know is that I don't want to be your deputy no more."

Big Bill nodded wistfully and said, "Well, like I said, it's a free country. But would you be willing to at least finish out your first two weeks?"

Taylor shook his head and said, "I don't need to stick around till payday. The town's welcome to any back wages I may have coming for the little I've done here."

Big Bill blew smoke out both nostrils and growled, "I ain't talking about anything you might have done so far. I'm talking about the mortal fix you'll be putting me in if you run out on me afore I can get some serious backup, damn it."

Taylor arched an eyebrow and asked what he was jawing so wild about. So Big Bill explained, "I'd have never recruited you if I had another deputy worth spit. Rightly or wrongly, I just gunned a bad Texican with a rep, and wrongly, in my opinion, another Texas herd is due before the end of this very week. You saw, the first night you got here, what dangersome fools some Texicans can be when they're likkered up and looking for an excuse to pick a fight with anyone handy."

Taylor nodded understandingly and said, "I did, and I reckon I owe you for that as well. But them old boys were just rawhiding me for the hell of it. They never took me for a gun-slick with a rep like your'n, Big Bill. Hell's bells, how many run-of-the-mill trail hands are about to go up against a man like *you*, drunk or even just plain *loco*?"

The older lawman stared off into space as he muttered, "Nobody can rightly say what any *loco* gent might do. Me and my trusty old Buntline Special can likely deal with any face-to-face trouble. But I ain't got eyes in the back of my head, and more than one good gun hand has been shot in the back by a sneak who was afraid to fight him fair and square, you know."

Taylor smiled thinly and said, "I've noticed that in my travels. I reckon it's fair when you get a man to turn around after you have the drop on him, huh?"

Big Bill shrugged and said, "You've already made known your views on the informal execution of Grat Lewis. I'm talking a real back shooting. I'm asking you to stay and watch my back just a few more days. Just till I can find another deputy as good as you."

Taylor didn't answer. Big Bill tried, "I could have left you to face the whole damned 808 outfit alone that time. I can't say it was fun getting to know you that way, Matt."

It worked. Taylor picked up the brass star from the desk between them, muttering, "I ought to see a head doctor. Lord knows there has to be something wrong with my head. But I reckon I owe you a few more days at least."

But as he pinned the deputy badge back on, Taylor warned the older man firmly, "Just till that outfit you're worried about passes through. After that you'll be on your own, whether you can find another backup as dumb as me or not, hear?"

Big Bill laughed boyishly and replied, "Don't get your bowels in an uproar so early, Matt. If that outfit heading our way is half as tough as it's supposed to be, they'll likely kill us both and we won't have to argue about it no more."

* * *

Despite a certain tenseness in the air he knew he could be imagining, the next few days passed so quietly that Taylor would have found them tedious had not he suspected it was a lull before a storm. Partly to keep himself busy and partly because he was sincerely interested in the way the world around him worked, the transplanted Texan spent most of the time getting to know the little trail town. Big Bill and Taylor's fellow deputies, Tim Hogan and Joe Walsh, seemed content to let Freewater take care of itself unless somebody yelled for help. The marshal himself was given to odd spells of invisibility when he wasn't at his desk or holding court at the Prairie Dog. Hogan and Walsh let Taylor patrol the few streets on his own if that was his fancy. Big Bill posted no duty roster and gave few orders as to who ought to be watching what. But Taylor was naturally curious and too active by nature to just sit around spitting and whittling with the boys.

He'd passed through many a town like Freewater in his time. But he'd seldom spent much time in any. His new job gave him a socially acceptable excuse to nose about and ask questions no cowhand, just passing through, would have gotten away with. His knowledge of the beef industry gave him as good a grasp on the way a cow town worked as a formal class in city planning might have, whether he knew it or not. He'd never thought to wonder before how towns wound up where they were.

The gently rolling shortgrass prairie that surrounded the town itself, and made up most of Freewater Township as well, gave no obvious clues as to why the compact cluster of frame structures lay here instead of, say, yonder, where that sunflower windmill was pumping lazy on the horizon. But as many a Utopian sect had already discovered in other parts, towns don't work planted just anywhere.

Freewater, as its name indicated once one thought about it, had sprouted a dozen or so years back because the site was the only place for a day's drive north or south where an all-summer trickle of spring water crossed the Ogallala Cattle Train. The trail hadn't just happened, either. Drovers could get in all sort of trouble driving cows just any old way. So the federal government regulated such interstate commerce by setting aside such strips of land as it wanted homesteaded, grazed as open range for a modest fee, or trampled to dust by cows on their way to market. The Ogallala Train had been created by the Bureau of Land Management, Department of the Interior, in the year of our Lord 1880. By then, having some grim experience with the confusion between cows and fence lines, they'd sagely run the official trail, north of the Indian Nation, smack along the string-straight state line dividing Colorado from Kansas, because few, if any, homesteaders were likely to string barbwire in a manner to pay the mighty confusing tax bills that would have resulted from owning, say, a hundred acres in Kansas and sixty in Colorado.

For once Washington had gotten things right. By the nineties the earlier and better-known trails to both the east and west had been closed by statute law or become just too vexed by barbwire to be practical. So towns along the one good trail left were thriving better than ever.

The founding fathers of Freewater had begun by damming the wash and erecting a saloon at the same time. The dammed wash had become a small prairie lake in no time. The water and soon bare cattle-and-camping grounds south of the water were provided for the asking, gratis, by Freewater Township. Everything else in town cost as much as the market would bear. The owners of the herds got a good deal. The merchants of the town made out as well or better. Many a forty-dollar-a-month cowhand was inclined to feel abused and resentful after a dusty day in the saddle when he discovered they wanted a whole damn nickel for a plain old beer or that the fancy gals of Freewater expected a whole day's wages for a mighty short favor, and that was why trail-town lawmen were expected to walk tall and talk tough.

The town needed the cowhands as much or more than the cowhands needed the town. But both sides found the other annoying. For if the trail herders felt the city slickers were taking advantage of them, the townsfolk saw little profit in having their streetlights and windows shot out by uncouth rustics. The ideal visit by a big outfit involved a fine balance between keeping just enough law and order to avoid serious property damage while, at the same time, allowing the boys to have enough fun to encourage them to come back again next year. The average day's drive for beef on the hoof was no more than twenty miles, and trail stops tended to be closer together than that. So by timing the stops as they drove, the drovers could leapfrog a stuffy stop that treated 'em mean, and they did, as many a town more prim and proper than Freewater had discovered to its chagrin.

Matt Taylor, as an experienced trail driver, had known to begin with why some trail stops were more popular with the boys than others. But conversing with the folk of Freewater as he made his rounds gave him a new perspective on the subject of law and order versus a good time. He hadn't suspected it could be so complicated. There was, for example, the matter of Freewater Fannie and her gals. He'd assumed, at first, their sordid trade was as legal as, say, the Prairie Dog Saloon, and from a practical point of view, it was. Freewater Fannie's house of ill repute was not the only such establishment in town, and the town law obviously policed that end of town, and yet, on paper, it didn't.

Incorporated by the state of Colorado, the six-by-six-mile square of the township lay officially on that side of the state line, just to the west of the federal cattle trail, with its main street running east and west so the boys could swing off said trail, either way, in search of such pleasures as they had the wherewithal to pay for. The red-light district and a couple of gambling hells that should have been ashamed of themselves actually lay in Kansas, thus immune from the city charter's regulations against whoring, opium, or professional gambling. But since the nearest Kansas county seat or sheriff's department lay a full day's ride to the east, Big Bill and his deputies were expected to keep just enough decorum on both sides of the state line to prevent outright murder or, worse yet, arson. For, in theory, any peace officer, anywhere, had the right to prevent an actual crime in progress, whether it was taking place within his jurisdiction or not. When the bemused Taylor asked for a more precise explanation of his duties at that end of town, Big Bill seemed to find them vague as well. He said, "To tell the truth, I've never had to haul a whore or tinhorn afore Judge Carver; I suspicion he prefers not to notice they're there. The regulars down that way know their place and try not to cause us trouble. Of course, should some drunk cowboy take to beating up one of the gals serious, I'll expect you to lay him out and haul him here to lockup, like anyone else who's disturbing the peace. The judge usually lets 'em off with a modest fine and a good scolding, once they sober up."

But Taylor insisted, "How? I mean how can a Colorado justice of the peace fine a man for disturbing the peace in Kansas, for Pete's sake?"

Big Bill explained, "Easy. No matter where you arrest an old boy on drunk and disorderly, he's still drunk and disorderly when you lock him up in Colorado, ain't he?"

Matt Taylor decided not to worry about it. He didn't intend to be there long enough to become an expert on the finer points of law. He had mighty mingled feelings about both his boss and his temporary job, and he hadn't gotten to know anyone else in town that well. All told, there were no more than four hundred regular residents of Freewater, counting women and children, and like most such tightly knit communities, they were inclined to be clannish until they got to know an unknown quality better. Taylor noticed that even at the boardinghouse where he was staying, none of the other boarders had much to say to him at mealtimes, even though he tried to mind his table manners and didn't smoke in bed.

By his second or third day in Freewater he'd of course gained some grasp on how the folk who just *had* to talk to him ran the town. Most of them doubled in brass. Neither the mayor and his town council nor any other official save for Big Bill Burton and his deputies could hope to live on their modest public services alone. Hence the rather pompous Judge Carver was more a notary and a lawyer when he wasn't called to hold court in the Methodist church, weekdays, or the one-room schoolhouse should a serious case come before him of a Saturday. He naturally never held trial on the Sabbath.

There were said to be two doctors in town, one an elderly gent with a drinking problem who mostly looked after the soiled doves of the red-light district, and the other a more respected member of the community who looked after decent folk. The one undertaker in Freewater spent most of his time as a wagon wright, for the local climate was healthy when no herd was in town. The schoolteacher, a handsome, albeit sort of severe-looking, blonde who was likely a Scandihoovian gal, ran the small town library from late afternoon to early evening with longer hours on Saturday. Most of the city council owned local businesses, from general store to the licensed saloons, while the mayor himself, a pudgy little cuss who smiled a lot, ran the one bank in town, which was no doubt why he'd been elected mayor to begin with. Shopkeepers and the hands at the livery stable and smithy just inside the proper city limits had begun to howdy or at least to nod to Taylor by the time he'd learned all this. But though he nodded back just as politely, he made no real effort to get friendlier with folk he didn't expect to know much longer. He'd already discovered that, as many a soldier or lawman could have told him, prowling about with a gun in hopes of heading off trouble could get dull as hell, and he could hardly wait to be on his way, once he'd fulfilled his agreement to stay out his two weeks as a town deputy. It hardly seemed possible, strolling the streets of such a sleepy little settlement, that anything really exciting was ever likely to happen again.

Many an old soldier or lawman could have told him that trouble was like that. It seldom came when one was expecting it. Hence, as Taylor reported for work Thursday morning to find Big Bill's desk deserted and Tim Hogan listlessly braiding a leather quirt while seated on the doorstep, trouble seemed the last thing on anyone's mind in Freewater. Taylor asked the junior deputy where the boss might be and whether he'd left any orders for anyone.

Tim shrugged and said, "I reckon Big Bill's sleeping late at Freewater Fannie's place. Him and her are old pals. As to orders, you can see for yourself that nary a tumbleweed is disturbing the peace right now."

Taylor stared morosely up the dusty deserted street. Some of the shops were opening up, and somewhere in the distance someone was hammering nails. But there were no riders or wheeled vehicles in motion. He grimaced and said, "I fear we're in for a mighty warm day for this late in the fall. May as well stretch my legs afore it gets too sultry for strolling."

Tim Hogan didn't argue. Taylor head on up Main Street, on the shadier south side. He'd have used the plank walks under the storefront overhangs if there'd been more traffic. But since he had the flatter roadway to himself, he saw no reason to go up and down the steps at the end of each short business block. So he didn't.

As he reached the intersection where the brick front of Freewater Savings and Loan occupied the northwest corner, he saw four ponies tethered out front. He thought nothing of it. The bank was only there to serve its customers, and gents who could not afford to ride into town had no business visiting a bank to begin with. As he was about to cross the intersection, Taylor saw a young mother in a sunbonnet, leading a little boy in knee pants, crossing at right angles to him. If she was taking her kid to school, they were a mite late. Then, as he idly watched them, he heard a muffled roar of gunshots and went for his own weapon as the door of the bank burst open and four rascals with feed sacks over their heads came busting out all at once, six-guns smoking and yelling fit to bust!

Taylor was so taken aback that, even gun in hand, he just stood there for the moment. Then the moment passed as the woman out in the middle of the intersection started running with her kid, lost her grip on his hand, and wailed like a banshee when the kid hit the dust facedown and just lay there, bawling. As his mother ran back to him Taylor saw the masked men had already mounted up, with astounding speed, and were trying to ride around the confusion of flapping skirts and bawling kid. All but one of them, who just didn't seem to give a damn about women and children when he was in a hurry. So without taking time to think, Taylor blew him backward out of his saddle just as he ran over the mother and child. Then, since he still had the time as well as the range, Taylor nailed a second owlhoot between the shoulder blades as the other two vanished in the dusty haze they'd stirred up.

Taylor ran toward the woman knocked down by the first one's pony. Her kid was sitting up now, yelling for his mammy even though she lay right there, facedown, with her sunbonnet kicked off and blood streaking her messed-up auburn hair. Taylor kept his gun out as he dropped to one

knee to feel the unconscious woman's throat for a pulse. Her
heart was still beating. Taylor wasn't sure what he'd have
done about it if it hadn't been. He told the little boy that his
mammy was all right and that big boys weren't supposed to
cry. The kid kept crying anyway. By now others were
coming, from all directions. The pudgy mayor was first to
reach Taylor. His lower lip was trembling with outrage as he
blurted, "They just held up my bank! What are you going to
do about it?"

Taylor waved his gun muzzle at the nearest one he'd
downed and said, "I already done what I could. This lady is
hurt. I don't know how bad."

By this time the crowd had become coeducational. A
pretty brunette dressed Gibson Girl fashion, in a puffed
white blouse and dark blue button-sided skirt, dropped to
her knees on the far side of the injured woman. She hauled
the crying kid away from his prone parent and handed him
into the care of a more motherly looking gal in a calico
Mother Hubbard before she bent over, carefully parted the
unconscious woman's hair to expose the nasty scalp wound,
and murmured, "Oh boy, this is going to take at least a
dozen stitches. But first we'd better check for concussion."

As the pretty little thing proceeded to roll the victim on
her back, Taylor helped, but felt obliged to ask, "Do you
know what you're doing, miss? No offense, but I'd say this
lady needs a real doctor right now."

The brunette went on with her examination as she told
Taylor, "I am a doctor. Didn't you know, ah, Deputy?"

He gulped and replied, "I'm Matt Taylor. They did tell
me a Dr. H. R. Harris was the best sawbones in town. But
surely you can't be him."

She dimpled at him and replied demurely, "Sure I can.
I'm Helen Rebecca Harris, M.D. Are we going to have a
tedious discussion about my qualifications or are you going
to help me get this poor woman over to my clinic, damn
it?"

The mayor protested, "Hold on now, Miss Helen. This young lawman is supposed to go after them bank robbers, not take up *medicine* at a time like this!"

Taylor glanced up at the faces all around him, recognized a few, and said, "You, you, and you in the butcher's apron. I want you to help the doc and me get all the injured wherever Miss Helen here wants 'em took."

Then he got to his feet and strode toward the nearest man he'd put on the ground, with the pudgy mayor in tow bitching on and on about his money. Taylor hunkered down over the first mean rider he'd shot. The man was still alive enough to cuss when Taylor ripped the feed sack from his head. The face exposed was that of a mere boy in his early teens. But his eyes were old with hate, and he snarled through his blood-flecked lips, "My kin will pay you back for killing me, you bastard!"

Taylor opened the wounded youth's shirtfront, slapped away a resisting hand, and said, "You ain't dead yet, and by the way, my folk was married lawful, unlike your'n, I suspicion. How come you ran that poor gal down like that, you careless rascal?"

The surly wounded youth said, "She was in my way. I hope I kilt her, just the way my brothers are fixing to kill you. Us Redford boys stick together tight as ticks, see?"

Behind Taylor, the mayor protested, "Do something sensible, Deputy! Are you just going to jaw like a fool at him or pistol-whip my *money* out of him?"

Taylor growled, "Simmer down. You don't pistol-whip a kid with a bullet in his chest if you expect him to say much. Anyone can see he ain't got no money bags on him now. It might make more sense to keep him alive until he can tell us where your money might have went, see?"

The boy on the ground coughed blood and groaned, "Go to hell. I ain't telling you nothing about nothing, hear?"

Before Taylor could reply, they were joined by Helen Harris. She dropped to her knees again beside Taylor and said, "They're on their way with the woman and her little boy. What have we got here?" Then she parted the bloody shirtfront a little wider and answered her own question soberly with "Oh boy. You do know how to aim a gun, don't you, Deputy? I just had a look at the other one. You severed his spine and blew his heart apart with the same shot."

The one closer to hand moaned, "Oh no, not Nick, too! My kin are sure going to be upset by this cruel way you treat Nick and me, lawman." Then he smiled up at Helen Harris to add, "Howdy, pretty lady. Do you reckon there's anything you can do about this old chest of mine? It don't hurt so bad now. But I sure feel poorly just the same. How come it's getting dark so early? I thought it was morning when we rid in just now."

She told him, in a not unkind but matter-of-fact tone, "I'm afraid there's nothing I can do for you. You're bleeding to death inside. Would you like us to fetch you a minister while there's still time?"

The boy's already pallid face turned an ashier shade and his eyes widened as her words sunk in. But he stayed game enough to answer quietly, "I was never one for praying, and I'd just as soon talk to a pretty lady as a sky pilot, anyways. Are you married up or spoken for, pretty lady?"

The mayor muttered, "Oh, for God's sake!" But Helen Harris took one of the dying boy's hands in both of her own as she told him gently, "I'm a spinster woman, so far. Are you proposing or just trifling with my affections, sir?"

He started to laugh, coughed more blood instead, and then he just lay there, smiling up at her glassy-eyed. She let go his hand to shut his eyes for him as she murmured, "He's gone. There was nothing I could do for him."

Taylor swallowed and murmured, "I'd say you done

enough for him, considering what he was in life." Then he rose and helped her to her feet as well while the mayor almost shouted, "All right now, damn it! The dead and injured has been dealt with and I still don't have my money! What are you going to do about that, Deputy?"

Taylor shrugged and said, "Look for it, I reckon. I got his family name out of him and he allowed he robbed your bank with kin. Two of the same got away, for now. So the next suspects I mean to question would be the ponies the two I got was riding."

That was easy enough. Neither pony had gone far, and thoughtful bystanders had tethered both just down the street. So Taylor headed that way as Helen Harris headed the other, to see to the less seriously hurt woman at her nearby clinic.

The mayor and most of the crowd tagged along after Taylor, as if to keep an eye on him. As they reached the bay pony that had knocked the young mother down, they were met by Big Bill Burton, who smiled at Taylor and said, "I just heard. You done me proud, old son. The money wasn't on this bay. You're barking up the wrong horse."

Taylor stared past the bay to where the grinning Tim Hogan was holding the reins of the paint the second one he'd shot had been riding. Two canvas bags were lashed to the horn of the paint's empty saddle. The mayor gasped, "Oh, thank God, that's it! That's the money they made our teller fork over!" Then he ran around the rump of the bay to grab at the money bags as if they were his long-lost children. As the pudgy little cuss ran for his bank to count out every penny, Big Bill smiled thinly at Taylor and said, "I don't know why, old son, but every time something like this happens, the damn fools insist on thanking God instead of us. Ain't life strange?"

Taylor sighed and said, "I have to credit the Lord or at least Lady Luck for some of what just happened. Had not I nailed the one called Nick, the money would have been long gone by now. I didn't really have time to pick and choose. Do you reckon I got the leader with that last lucky shot? If I did, his name might add up to the late Nick Redford. Might that mean much in these parts?''

Big Bill nodded soberly at him and said, ''There's no might about it. I can't say which of the Redford brothers might have called himself their leader. But all four are, or were, well known indeed in these and other parts. You mean you never heard of the Redford gang, Matt?''

Taylor shrugged and said, ''I told you when you hired me that I was new at the game. Are you saying I just nailed somebody important?''

Big Bill said he sure had, and Tim Hogan chimed in with, ''The Redfords is Colorado's answer to, say, the Daltons, down in the Indian Nation. You just made yourself some *bounty* money, Matt!''

Taylor smiled sheepishly and replied, ''All in all, I'd feel better if I'd won it in a roping contest. The younger one told me, as he was dying, that his brothers might come after me, personal, for spoiling their fun this morning.''

Big Bill sighed and said, ''There's no might about it, old son. They're *sure* to come after you, once they've had time to lick their wounds and do some planning. By nightfall the whole world will know the name of the man as wiped out half the gang this morning. But don't you worry, Matt. Me, the boys, and my old Buntline Special will be there to back you up.''

Less than an hour later, as Matt Taylor made his way to the lady doctor's clinic, he could see he was already sort of famous, and it took some getting used to. Folk who up to now had sort of smiled through him had commenced to greet him like they had him down as a cousin or closer in the family Bible. His newfound friends didn't bother him half as much as the thought of the *enemies* he'd just made. For he knew that even if he just rode on now, he'd have a time living down the simple fact that he'd always be known as the man who'd faced up to the Redford boys, one against four, and won.

He knew what had happened to old John Wesley Hardin in El Paso just a year or so ago. The fact that Hardin had moved away from his old haunts and tried to stay out of trouble hadn't helped a bit when a two-bit braggart called Johnny Selman had seen the chance to embellish his own rep by blowing Hardin's brains out in the Acme Saloon, from the back. As noted gun-slicks had known since Cockeyed Jack McCall shot James Butler Hickok in the back back in '76, a man with a rep needed eyes in the back of his head or friends to watch his back. He was beginning to understand the anxieties of Big Bill Burton better. It made him nervous as hell.

At the clinic, a modest two-story frame building with living quarters above, Helen Harris let him in with a smile and led him through her waiting room, where a worried-looking young gent in the straw hat and bib overalls that most homesteaders favored was squirming about on a hard-wood bench as if he had worms. In the back, in a bedstead made of steel tubing painted white, lay the young mother who'd been run down in front of the bank. Her head was swathed in bandages, and the lady doc had her down to her shimmy under the muslin sheet. Helen murmured, "She's going to be all right. She's about recovered from the concussion, but I want to be sure before I let her man carry her home."

The girl in the bed fluttered her lashes and asked for her little boy. Helen told her soothingly, "Jimmy is over at your sister's house here in town, Mrs. Keller. Your husband and I agreed that was the best place for the boy, for now."

That made her ask for someone called Big Jim. So Helen

told her, "He's right outside, dear. If I bring him in, will you promise not to excite yourself? You've had quite a trying time this morning, you know."

The injured girl, for she was little more than that, sighed and murmured, "I know. I got kicked by a horse. I was so afraid they'd hurt my baby. Are you sure he's all right?"

Helen assured her her man could tell her that and asked Taylor to keep an eye on the girl as she went to fetch the man. When she left, the girl on the bed stared up at him, out of focus, and repeated, "I was kicked by a horse, you know," to which he replied softly, "I know. I was there. I saw the way you tried to shield the boy with your own body. You're a mighty brave woman, Mrs. Keller."

She sighed and said, "No I'm not. I'm a mother. That's what mothers are supposed to do."

Helen came back with the young nester. He'd removed his hat, and his eyes were red-rimmed as he stared thoughtfully at Taylor and said, "I'm sorry, sir. I didn't know who you was until the doc told me just now." He started to move around to his wife's side. Then he suddenly stuck out his hand and sobbed, "God bless you, Matt Taylor. We won't be forgetting what you done this day!"

Taylor shook with the man. He had to. But then he said, "Aw, mush. Your woman was the one as saved the boy."

Helen took Taylor by the other arm and told Keller, "We'll be in the next room if you need us. I expect you to give a holler if she tries to sit up again." Then she told Taylor, "Come on, I think we could both use a little medication."

She led him into her next-door office, waved him to a window seat, and produced a bottle of medicinal alcohol from the top drawer of a filing cabinet, saying, "It's the otherwise useless coloring and flavoring that stinks up your breath and leaves you hung over. I prefer to do my serious drinking with surgical precision, don't you?"

He chuckled and said, "I can't say. I don't drink with surgeons all that often."

She laughed, found two glass tumblers as well, and poured them both heroic shots. She handed his to him, sat down on a nearby hardwood stool, and said, "Bottoms up. Are you always this calm or are you still in shock?"

He sipped at his raw alcohol. It took some getting used to. He wheezed and muttered, "Good stuff. I didn't know I was supposed to go into shock. I didn't get hit by nothing."

She nodded and asked, "How do you feel, then? I don't get many chances to examine the winner after a gunfight."

He started to shrug her question off. Then he stared at her soberly and said, "You're good, Doc. I thought I was acting all right. But to tell the truth, I *do* feel mighty odd right now."

She sipped her own drink, more courageously, and said, "Tell me about it, Matt."

He tried to. He said, "The oddest thing is what I don't feel. I mean, I never killed a man before, and the other night, when I was just watching a man *get* killed, it made me feel just awful. I've had plenty of fights in my time. I've even swapped shots, with less grim results, before. But I always figured, if I really wound up killing someone really *dead*, I'd feel . . . well, *different*. Maybe good, maybe bad, but not like now, not feeling all that *anything*. It's almost as if it never happened, or it happened to somebody else entire. Do you reckon I'm just a cold-blooded killer at heart, Miss Helen?"

She shook her head and said, "No. I think you're perfectly normal. My father served as a Union army surgeon during the war. He never talked about it much, before he saw I was following in his footsteps, and seemed more willing to share his medical experiences with a girl child. Dad was very interested in the way some men cracked up in battle while others, who'd seen as much or more action, didn't. He said he'd noticed that the men who seemed the most emotional, either way, were the ones more apt to get in trouble."

"What did he mean by either way?" asked Taylor uncertainly.

She said, "Oh, you know, carrying on as if they'd done something wonderful or, contrarywise, carrying on about how guilty they felt about doing what they'd had to do. Dad said the ones who apologized the most about killed Johnny Reb were often the ones who'd seen no action at all. We're all taught that one's supposed to feel guilty at such times. So many a man just making up war stories feels obliged to throw that in. Dad said most of the normal soldiers he'd talked to about it felt just the way you say you do. Neither guilt nor glory."

He sipped some more alcohol and decided, "That's about the size of it. I'm sure glad I'm not crazy, Miss Helen. To tell the truth, I was starting to wonder about it."

She nodded and said, "You're going to be all right, Matt. You can't be what people call a cold-blooded killer. They're the ones who feel *big* about it afterwards. As Dad always said and as I've learned in my own practice, killing a human being is not too difficult. Sometimes they die on you no matter how hard you try to save them. That's the hard job, *saving* life, not *taking* it."

He arched an eyebrow at her to ask quietly, "Does it make you feel like a big shot when you save a life, Miss Helen?"

She nodded firmly and said, "You bet your hide it does. It makes me feel ten feel tall, even if I am sort of short next to most men. Even my dad told me there was little future in medicine for a mere she-male. But I made it through medical school, hazing and all, and I *have* saved patients' lives, more than once, and I don't mind saying I feel proud as a peacock about that."

He said, "You ought to, I reckon. Is that how come you're out here doctoring sick folk? I mean, you being a woman and all."

She nodded and said, "It is. It's not easy, getting folk to accept you as a real physician, even out west. But we all have to do what we were made to do, right?"

He frowned and said, "I ain't sure. I thought I was meant to be a top hand, until recent. I just took this infernal job as a lawman up sort of temporary. But at the rate I'm going, I'm likely to get stuck with this dumb career."

She shook her head and said, "You can't mean that, Matt. You may or may not be a fine cowboy. But I know for a fact you're a good lawman, and such help is a lot harder to find."

He protested, "Any gent who don't mind walking can be a small-town lawman. I don't know about Big Bill Burton hisself, but I suspect I could show the other deputies a thing or two about turning a stampede in a hailstorm. You got to know an awful lot to work with cows."

She insisted, "You have to know an awful lot to do anything at all well, Matt. A lot of men know how to fight, and even more men know how to run from one. You handled that bank robbery just right this morning, and as I just said, such help can be hard to find."

He put the rest of his drink aside, muttering, "One thing's for sure; I know I can't outdrink you *mano a mano*, Doc. As for what happened this morning, I just happened to be there. Big Bill would have likely nailed all four of 'em if he'd been there."

She shrugged and asked, "Why *wasn't* he there, then?" And while he knew, and suspected she knew, too, he could only say, "Nobody can be everywhere at once. Like I said, I just got lucky."

She said, "Oh, sure you did. A well-known gang of

outlaws rides into town in broad daylight, and only one deputy on a four-man force bothers to notice?"

He didn't answer. He didn't like the drift of her comments at all. But how was one to say Big Bill hadn't been in on the bank robbery without accusing him of sleeping on duty in a whorehouse? He had to admit that, either way, she'd made an interesting point.

The big outfit they'd been worrying about rode in that Saturday, just as the local hands from surrounding spreads rode in to celebrate payday. It was obviously a lethal combination, but to Taylor's surprise and relief, nothing much seemed to be happening as hands wearing their hats Colorado or Texas crowded into town around sundown. He noticed that no matter whether it was Big Bill or himself who paused in a saloon doorway for a look-see, everyone got sort of quiet. He was too modest to assume word had gotten around already. He was simply sincerely pleased to see the concerns expressed by Big Bill appreared groundless.

He wasn't aware how seriously he'd taken talk about a tough outfit until, as he turned from the doorway of the Bull-Head near the east end of Main Street, he heard his name called and spun around in an instinctive gunfighting crouch to face the two men standing there, hands polite as they smiled at him warily. They were both dressed cow, and sort of trail-dusted. One was a kid with a lopsided grin and a shock of hair down his forehead. The other was a mite older and darker, with Latin features but as Anglo-talking as any other Texan as he said, "Hold your fire, pard. We're on your side. This here's young Will Rogers from the Indian Nation. I'd be Charly Siringo, and no, I ain't a Mex. My mother hailed from Ireland and my dad was Eye-talian. I'm just Texican my own self."

Taylor nodded and said, "I've heard tell of you, Mr. Siringo. You'd be a range detective, right?"

The somewhat sinister-looking but amiable enough thief hunter said, "Call me Charly. Me and Will here has been trying to track down a mess of purloined cows, stolen off the Indian agency at Fort Reno."

Will Rogers added, "Beef meant to feed the South Cheyenne. All wearing Uncle Sam's brand. So far, us Cherokee haven't lost any, but us redskins got to stick together."

Taylor cocked an eyebrow at the young hand and said, "We ain't going to get far if you keep greening me, kid. You ain't no more an Indian than I am."

Young Rogers smiled sheepishly and said, "Well, I got *some* Cherokee blood, damn it. Is it my fault half the Indian Nation has been opened up to both sides of the family? The parts that ain't been incorporated into the new territory of Oklahoma are still Indian enough, and them poor South Cheyenne are getting robbed blind."

Taylor said, "I don't know what I can do to help. But what say we go inside and talk sitting down with some suds?"

The two thief hunters agreed, and as the three of them went back in the Bull-Head and headed for a corner table, it was cleared for them as if by magic. As the three of them sat down, Siringo chuckled quietly and said, "I admire a man who can scare Texas hands so easy. Does a town this size really need two lawmen as ferocious as you and old Bill Burton? All at once, I mean. No offense, but I've seen one gent with a rep keep a town this size under control."

As a waitress in a shocking skirt came over to take their orders, Taylor explained, "I didn't have a rep until just recent, and to tell the truth, we was expecting more trouble from this bunch."

Siringo waited until the gal had them down for three

schooners and a pitcher of draft before he said dryly, "We heard about you and them two Redford boys. I can watch the crowd good enough from where I'm sitting. But if you don't mind a tip from a man who's seen the elephant in his time, you'd best make sure you keep your back to the corner in the future."

Taylor shrugged and said, "Thanks, I wasn't worried *enough* about such matters till you boys showed up. I've been studying on that stolen beef you mentioned. So far I've seen two herds passing through. Neither was branded US or BIA."

Will Rogers said, "They'd be branded US. First choice goes to the soldiers at Fort Reno. The government buys it for both the army and the South Cheyenne at the same time, see?"

The gal brought the schooners and pitcher to their table. So Taylor poured as he mused, "Can't say I've read either brand in recent memory. What gave you boys the notion I could help you?"

Siringo reached for his drink, saying, "Grat Lewis. An old boss of your'n who wound up dead in this fair city. He sure was an eely rascal, and they wanted him in Fort Smith for running off with Indian beef, as I recall."

Taylor nodded and said, "I don't doubt it. He sure robbed everyone else he could. But you boys are way off base if you think Lewis passed this way with recently stole cows. I rode with him, and the herd, all the way up to Nebraska. It was a consolidated herd, made up in the Panhandle. They wore many a brand, but since I must have chased every infernal one of 'em at one time or another, I can tell you they was all branded pure Texican. It was the trail boss who was the crook, not the stockmen who contracted with Lewis for the drive."

Charly Siringo sipped some suds, put the schooner back down, and asked quietly, "How come you killed him, then?"

Taylor forced himself to meet the range detective's calm but mighty interested stare. It wasn't easy. Taylor was glad he'd never stolen one cow as he replied, "It had nothing to do with Indian beef. Grat ran off with the payroll after he had no more use for me and the boys."

Will Rogers said flatly, "I can see why you thought it only right to kill the rascal, then."

Siringo said nothing. Taylor sipped some beer to wet down his suddenly dry mouth before he said, "I may be able to save us all a lot of needless jawing if I knew for certain you boys was only after cow thieves and nobody else."

Siringo almost purred as he assured Taylor quietly that he wasn't there to enforce any Colorado or Kansas regulations. So Taylor nodded and said, "Well, since honesty is the best policy when one can get away with it, I was trying to bring Lewis in for questioning about pure theft when he sort of got into an argument with Big Bill Burton and, ah, lost."

Siringo enjoyed a slow sip of beer before he nodded and said, half to himself, "Why, sure. I can see that cur dog, Lewis, slapping leather on a man of Burton's rep as if it was happening before my very eyes. I take it old Bill used that long-donged whatever he's so proud of?"

Taylor nodded and said, "Buntline Special. You've no doubt heard the tale of how he come by such a wondrous weapon?"

Siringo grimaced and said, "Many, many times. I can picture that grand ceremony in the Long Branch in my mind's eye as well."

Will Rogers chimed in with, "Oh, I heard about that. Didn't that writer gent give one of them special guns to old Heck Thomas as well?"

Siringo said, "I wasn't there. But I doubt it. Old Heck had no business in Dodge to begin with. He still works for Judge Parker, out of Fort Smith, and the last time I seen

him, he was packing a sensible six-gun like everybody
else."

Taylor asked cautiously, "Are you saying Big Bill might
not be all he's cracked up to be, Charly?"

Siringo laughed easily and replied, "Hell, *I* ain't all I'm
cracked up to be. The only lawman I've yet to meet who
lives up to his rep, total, would be Marshal Bill Tilghman,
down in Perry. He ain't as famous as a lot of us. It may well
be because he brings most of his men in alive. Most come
quiet, for the pure and simple reason that Tilghman is the
no-bull real thing. Once *he* comes after you, you got two
choices. You can put up your hands or you can die. There
ain't no way any man born of woman can expect to *beat* that
hardcased hairpin. It's been tried by some of the best, with
fatal results."

Will Rogers said, "I heard he was good, too. But what's
to stop someone from gunning even a man like Tilghman in
the back?"

Siringo shrugged and said, "That's been tried, too.
Maybe someday somebody will. But it won't be *this* child. I
don't mind saying that I'd hate like hell to go up against
Marshal Tilghman."

"What about our own Big Bill Burton?" Taylor found
himself asking, even as he wished he hadn't.

Charly Siringo shrugged and said, "Since we're both on
the same side of the law, why worry about it? It's been nice
talking to you, Matt. But me and the kid had best get it on
up the road. If they get that Indian beef sold and skinned out
afore we catch 'em, well, we ain't likely to catch 'em."

Taylor saw them to the door. He had no use for a pitcher
of beer himself. As the two thief catchers strode off toward
the livery, a couple of young cowhands were already
helping themselves to the abandoned beer. Some old boys
just had no shame, or mayhaps they were already broke.
The fancy gals across the state line charged scandalous

prices when this many horny young gents were in town all at once.

Taylor walked that way, since that was the direction trouble was most apt to start after nightfall. As if to prove great minds ran in the same channels, Big Bill hailed him from the far side of the street. When Taylor joined him in the doorway of a hat shop closed for the night, Big Bill muttered, "Showdown coming. Just got the word from one of Freewater Fannie's fancy dans. Seems a couple of big bad squirts have been announcing their intentions to have it out with me this evening."

Taylor whistled and asked, "Do you reckon it could be the Redford brothers, boss?"

To which Big Bill replied calmly, "I doubt it. They'd be after *you*. I suspicion I know who the poor idjets would be. I told you I'd had trouble with this outfit before. The last time they come through, I had to bust a few heads. Most of 'em took it like sports after they'd sobered up in the morning. But a mean young Anglo and an even meaner Mex made some war talk, cold sober, as we was letting 'em ride on without their guns. They promised they'd get some more guns and that I'd best watch out the next time they rode in with the Circle Bar. So they have and I'm watching out. I got Joe Walsh staked out across from Freewater Fannie's. He'll signal when he sees 'em heading this way. There ain't nothing open along Main Street betwixt here and trail gap between the good and evil part of town. So I got six in the wheel and we shall see what we shall see."

Taylor said, "I just talked to Charly Siringo in the Bull-Head. He could still be in town if I hurry."

Big Bill shook his head and said, "I need you here to watch my back more than I need old Charly Siringo doing anything. Did he say what he was here for, Matt?"

"He did. Him and a kid sidekick are hunting cows stole down in the Indian Nation. I couldn't help him. So the last I saw of him, albeit just a minute ago, he was headed on up the Ogallala. I'm sure I could still catch up with him, and there can't be two cow waddies on this earth who'd face up to you and Charly Siringo!"

This time Big Bill's voice was downright surly as he insisted, "Forget it. Old Charly had no right to pass through my town without paying me a courtesy call. Don't never do that if and when you find yourself wearing a badge in another lawman's town, old son. It's a good way to get yourself killed by accident. But even if that rude dago wasn't so rude, I wouldn't want him mixing in on what's about to happen. Did I want them boys to back down, I'd just have to face 'em down with you and Tim Hogan to either side of me. I got Tim across the way on a rooftop with a Winchester, by the way. I'll want you to stay here under the overhang and out of easy sight when the balloon goes up."

Taylor frowned up at the taller man and protested, "That ought to work. But, no offense, it looks more like pure murder than a balloon to me. Why can't we just throw down on 'em from all sides and take 'em alive?"

Big Bill shrugged and said, "We could, but to what avail? On what charge? Getting drunk and talking big to a mess of whores? Judge Carver would just let 'em go again, and this is already getting tedious. I aim to settle the matter once and for all, tonight."

Taylor thought and chose his words before he announced flatly, "I'll stand at your side and back your play, fair and square, as needlessly severe as it sounds to me. I won't skulk here in the shadows and ambush 'em in a cross fire with Hogan. I ain't no damn Apache, but like the Indian chief said, I have spoken."

Big Bill chuckled fondly and asked, "Is that what you figured I had in mind, old son? I never mentioned no Apache tricks. When we get the signal I mean to step out in the middle of the street, alone, to await their pleasure. That'll put my back to most of this fool town, and the boys

I'll be facing rode in with a big outfit. Any gunplay is sure to bring a mess of folk running, and that's where you and Tim come in. You're to wave 'em all back and Tim's to pick off anyone who starts up with you. I don't want *you* shooting into a crowd at ground level. Lord knows who you might hit, a block up the street, that way, savvy?''

Taylor pictured the likely near future in his mind's eye and said grudgingly, "All right, forget what I said about murder. But you sure seem to like things complexicated. If it was me, I'd take 'em alive with mayhaps a side trip to Fist City before the judge ever saw them in the morning. Spending nights in a steel box with a busted nose can get to be a tedious experience that few old boys with a lick of sense would care to risk repeating.''

Big Bill smiled grimly and said, "Your delicate manners does you credit, Matt. But if those two pistol punks had a lick of sense to begin with, we wouldn't be having this conversation. I'm older than you, not crueler, old son. There's nasty drunks you can haul in polite, and then there's them you can't. Young Ben Fuller and his pal, Pancho Robles, has offered to kill me, more than once, in front of witnesses. I still meant to leave the first move up to them. But I sure don't feel bound to keep this fool war going until I *lose*. So I have spoken, too.''

Taylor didn't know how to answer that. He was saved from the thankless chore of having to when, in the distance, they could both hear the tinny clatter of someone beating on a pan with a spoon. Taylor didn't think many noisy kids would still be up at this hour. So he didn't comment. But Big Bill still said, "That's old Joe's signal. Fuller and Robles are coming. It's about time.''

Then he hauled his long-barreled Buntline Special out his waistband as if he were a schoolteacher getting ready to cane an unruly student with a yardstick, and turned from Taylor to march out to the center of the dimly lit and dusty street, facing the deeper darkness to the east with the sixteen-inch barrel of his famous gun down the side of his famous right leg. It looked fair and mayhaps a mite suicidal to Taylor. It was only in the pulp-paper penny dreadfuls that a man who knew in advance that trouble was coming was supposed to be dumb enough to leave his sidearm in its holster. Holsters were meant to carry your gun when you were not using it. It seemed highly unlikely the two toughs coming would be packing their six-guns anywhere but in their hands.

A million years went by. Then two barely visible figures could be seen side by side and still striding, in step, up the center of the street. They spotted the lone figure of Big Bill about the same time and stopped about thirty yards east of him. It was easy shouting and tricky pistol range. Taylor would have moved a lot closer if it had been him facing a man with a pistol that shot like a carbine. One of them called out, "Is that you, Marshal?" And when Big Bill announced it sure was, the other let fly one of those rooster laughs vaqueros went in for when they were feeling ferocious and jolly at the same time.

Big Bill waited until the string of Spanish cussing that followed the crowing died down before he called back, "That sounded mighty pretty, greaser. Now I want you boys to reach for the stars with empty hands or fill the same with your guns so's I can fill you with lead. I don't care either way. So the choice is your own."

The Anglo called Fuller yelled back, "We got our guns handy, Marshal; are you still packing that freak Colt you pistol-whipped me with the last time?"

Big Bill answered jovially, "I sure am. Are you fresh brats afeared I have the range on you? Well, never let it be said I wasn't a good sport." And then he started walking toward them, his gun still pointed at the ground, as from the shadows, Taylor gasped and murmured, "Oh no! That's just plain stupid!"

Naturally, Big Bill didn't hear him, and as Taylor watched, the big man already facing big odds marched toward his enemies down the center of the street as if he owned it.

A few thundering seconds later he did. Fuller took one step backward, and then, seeing a mere Mex was standing his ground, Fuller dropped into a fighting crouch and fired. Robles got off two rapid-fire rounds as well before Big Bill simply swung his big gun up, shoulder-high, to aim down the long barrel as he put them both on the ground with exactly two shots.

Then, as Big Bill had warned, doors and windows commenced to pop open and Main Street filled with a herd of men pouring out of doorways on both sides. Matt Taylor ran out to the center to face the oncoming mob with his own gun drawn and his back to Big Bill and the aftermath of his short but noisy fight. Taylor fired a shot in the air to gain their undivided attention before he yelled, "That's far enough, gents. The war's over and the law has things under control down this way. So let's all keep back lest you stampede the evidence, hear?"

A townie who recognized Taylor called back from the crowd, "What's going on Matt?" to which Taylor replied, "Nothing. I just told you it was over. So stay put and let's keep it that way, hear?"

Then Big Bill was by his side, roaring, "You heard my deputy. I got me a dead Mex and a winged white boy to deal with. We'll want some help clearing the battlefield. Do I hear any volunteers?"

That got them to backing off pretty good. But Big Bill called out, "Jake Waterman, Mike Dillon, Windy Brown, haul your lazy bones right back here. I got a chore for you boys, and it's your own fault for being so damned nosy."

As the trio he'd dragooned drifted their way sheepishly, and the crowd drifted the other way muttering, Joe Walsh joined Big Bill and Taylor, a pair of gun belts draped over one arm and his gun in his free hand, to announce, "Ben Fuller says he's sure sorry and that he'd like to see his mother now. You got Robles smack through the heart. How come you didn't finish Fuller off, boss?"

Big Bill shrugged and replied, "That would have been spitesome, once he was down, facing state prison with a crippled gun arm. I don't like to kill anyone who don't really need to be killed, and I could see as I stood over him that he'd pissed his pants and no doubt seen the error of his ways."

Taylor had to grin as he pictured Big Bill looming over the shot-up troublemaker with a smoking gun and an undecided expression on his granite face. Big Bill turned to him and said, "Matt, you'd best go fetch Doc Harris and have her meet us at the lockup."

Taylor frowned thoughtfully and asked, "Wouldn't it be just as easy for us and easier for her if we carried him to her clinic? Joe just said he was disarmed and more interested in his mother than a fight."

Big Bill shook his head sternly and growled, "Fuller may or may not be spoiling for a fight with us now. But him and the Mex rode in with the Circle Bar. If even *half* the outfit feels at all upset about what just happened, we could be talking about an easy two dozen drunk and pissed-off Texicans. So do as I say, and if you see a crowd out front afore you can fetch the lady doc, just get her safe back home. Fuller entire ain't worth the risk of one hair on that sweet gal's head. So if his pals don't mind him dying, *I* surely don't give a shit."

When Taylor got to the clinic, he found Helen getting ready for bed. But since she'd thrown on a kimono to answer her door and since she was used to emergency calls as well, she just hauled on her high-buttoned shoes, picked up her black bag, and went with him in a no-nonsense state

of partial dishabille. He thought it mighty sporting of her to
leave her place without even taking the time to pin her hair
up proper. He thought she looked a lot handsomer with her
dark ringlets falling softly down over her shoulders, too.

As they swung the last corner to see the front of the
lockup ahead, they saw the street out front was still clear,
and lit up better than usual as well. Someone had thought to
hang coal oil lanterns along the hitching rail out front.
Taylor took Helen's arm and said, "All right. Let's make a
quickstep beeline, and if you hear me tell you to run, you're
to run back the way we just came, not for that front door,
hear?"

She nodded firmly and they broke cover to quickstep
what felt more like a country mile than the actual seventy-
five yards over lamplit open ground. The door opened for
them as they got there. It looked sort of spooky doing that
with no light coming from inside. But once they joined Big
Bill and the others in the unlit front office, they could see
fairly well by the light coming through the windows from
the lamps out front. Big Bill smiled down at Helen and said,
"It was mighty Christian of you to come, Miss Helen. The
winged gun-slick we got in the back ain't worth the time and
trouble of a Cheyenne medicine man. But I'd sort of like to
send him on to state prison alive."

Helen nodded and said, "Matt here told me all about it on
the way over. I'd best see how bad it is."

Leaving Tim Hogan and Joe Walsh on guard out front,
Big Bill led her back to the cell block, with Taylor tagging
along, invited or not. In one of the three side-by-side patent
cells lay a much younger kid than Taylor had pictured. He
was missing his shirt, and someone had stripped bedding
and mattress from the bare spring-straps of the fold-down
bunk he lay on. The cell was not too brightly illuminated by
a single candle in a bottle wedged between the front bars.
Helen wrinkled her nose and said, "I have to have more

light in here." So as Big Bill unlocked the door, he told
Taylor to fetch a lamp from out front. Getting there only
took him a few strides. But then he had to ask the other
deputies where a damned lamp might be. Joe Walsh said,
"In the sideboard, against yonder wall. I dasn't leave this
window."

At the other window, on the far side of the door, Tim
Hogan said, "Me neither. You reckon they'll really be
coming, Matt?"

Taylor said he didn't know as he hunkered down to haul a
brass lamp out, shook it to make sure there was oil in it, and
headed back to the cell block. He struck a match to light the
lamp along the way. It wasn't easy. It took four matches
before he had the wick adjusted right.

He carried it into Fuller's combined cell and emergency
ward to ask Helen Harris where she wanted it. She looked
up from where she knelt by the cot with her open bag at her
knees and asked him to stand over the head of the bunk with
it. So he did. As the brighter light shone down on the
wounded youth, he heard her sudden intake of breath. He
gasped a mite as well. For the wound was nastier than
anyone had call to expect from even a .45 round.

The lady M.D. asked Big Bill, "What did you shoot this
boy with, for heaven's sake?"

Big Bill shrugged modestly and said, "Hollow-point .45,
ma'am. It's a Hindu trick the Limey army larnt in a place
called Dum Dum. You drill a hole or cut an X in the front
end of the slug, and as you see, it slows your target down
considerable when it chews into him."

Taylor grimaced and said, "They came close to doing
you with the plain old bullets they was casting your way,
Big Bill. How come I seem to have been the only one there
who noticed that?"

Big Bill shrugged modestly and said, "They was shooting crazy-kid style. I took time to aim. It don't matter who

shoots how much first. What matters is who hits his target first, see?"

Helen swore under her breath and asked them both to hush. She explained, "I can barely see what I'm doing, and thanks to the wonders of modern ballistics, I have a lot more to do here. I have to get all these bits of shattered bone and chewed-up lead out before he snaps out of that opiate I just gave him. He failed to swallow half as much as I wanted him to. If the shock and the opiate wear off before I can back out, it's going to take the three of us to hold him down. Could you hold that lamp just a little closer, Matt?"

He could. Both men watched as she went on digging with her forceps. Big Bill opined it reminded him of picking seeds from a stomped-on watermelon. Taylor swallowed the green taste in his mouth and said, "You're fixing to get blood on the knees of your gown, Miss Helen. I seem to be standing in some at the moment."

She said, "I know. It goes with the job. Lemon juice and cold water will take it out later. How many chunks are one of your hollow points supposed to break into, Marshal?"

He said, "As many as possible. How does six or seven sound to you, ma'am? I've seldom had occasion to count. Since most of the time an old boy dies direct when I nails him with my old Buntline Special. How does this rascal's chances on living look to you, ma'am?"

She grimaced and said, "Awful. This shoulder will be stiff for as long as he lives, if he lives, and that's not likely if I leave any lead in him to poison him. So far I've found eight, and I'm running out of places to look, and oh, here's a nice bone splinter."

The pink shard of bone she hauled out with her forceps didn't look nice to Taylor. He said thoughtfully, "I've met a few old-timers still wandering about with bullets in 'em, Doc. It didn't seem to be doing them much harm."

She sniffed and said, "It could hardly have been doing

them much good, but it's true a lead bullet lodged in nothing worse than muscle tissue can encyst and not lead-poison one too much. This wound tore open a joint, and some lymph vessels as well. So we're talking lead poisoning with a captial *P*. On the other hand, I dasn't tear him open more than I've already had to. He's lost more blood than he can afford already, and I'd best start backing out and just pray I got all the metal out of him."

They both watched with interest as she first irrigated the wound again with her rubber bulb filled with alum water and started sewing all sorts of slimy pink things together before the wound could refill with blood. She sutured fast, with admirable skill, and still had to irrigate at least a dozen times before she got to where she was sewing outer hide with a short length of sterile goose quill sticking out to let the wound drain *when*, not *if*, it festered. Big Bill knew enough about bullet wounds of the era to opine, "Nice job. Now, if only the pus runs out more buttery- than mustard-colored, he ought to be fit to stand trail in a day or so."

She began to clean the youth's chest with alcohol-soaked lint as she amended that to, "More like two weeks if you're really in that much of a hurry. What will he be charged with, Marshal?"

Big Bill said, "I'm hoping for attempted murder. He told all sort of folk he meant to kill me, and I got witnesses to say he fired first. I sure wish I hadn't crippled his right arm, though. How's he supposed to make little rocks out of big ones, over at state prison, with only one left arm?"

Matt Taylor said, "We can clean up here, Miss Helen. You'd best let me carry you home now."

She stared blankly up at him to reply, "I can't leave yet. He hasn't even recovered from the opiate yet and—"

"Matt's right," Big Bill cut in, adding, "You've done more for him than he deserves, and for that I thank you, and the town will pay you as soon as you bill 'em. Meanwhile, this night is far from over, and I don't want you here if there's more trouble. Get her on home, Matt. I'll have Joe mop up in here."

She didn't like it much, but Taylor hauled her and her bag up anyway, saying soothingly, "I'll explain along the way, Miss Helen. But nobody here can say how much time we have left. So let's go."

He led her, still protesting, back out front. Tim Hogan opined the coast still looked clear as he opened the door for them. But Taylor didn't do much breathing until he had the she-male M.D. around a corner and they seemed to have the darker side street to themselves. As they slowed down, albeit not much, Helen, of course, demanded an explanation. He said, "I told you coming that Ben Fuller has lots of friends. Any friends that dead Mex had are apt to feel even *more* annoyed at us."

She nodded understandingly but said, "Surely the four of you should be able to hold them off from behind those strong walls."

He shook his head and said, "It won't be four before I get back to the three of 'em. Ben Fuller ain't on our side. As to the strong walls, they're balloon-frame. Pine two-by-fours betwixt cedar siding and plastered lath-wood. The only safe place in the fool building would be the patent cells. They got boilerplate walls. But no loopholes, and you may have noticed the sides facing the front door are only screened by bars. So our best bet will still be the front door and windows. I hope nobody's smart enough to shoot out all them hanging lanterns afore they make a serious rush."

She gulped and said, "Oh my God, can't you enlist some of the other men in town to help you, Matt?"

He shook his head and said, "They ain't paid to shoot it out with tough outfits. They pay us so they don't have to. Could you walk a mite faster, ma'am?"

She could, and did, but told him, "I don't want you going

back there, Matt. If that big bully and two deputies can't
hold off a mob, I fail to see how you dying with them can
possibly help."

He said, "I can't, either. But I have to look at my own
face in the mirror every time I shave. Big Bill and the boys
would never talk to me again if I let 'em get killed without
even trying to help. He ain't a bully, by the way. I ain't sure
just what he is, but tonight I watched him prove he was the
man he brags on being. I'd have never moved in like that
against two gents with their guns already out and even let
them fire first! You should have seen it, Doc."

She said, "I'm glad I didn't. I only like to observe
patients suffering mental problems when there may be
something I can do to help. Can't you see Marshal Burton is
psychotic, Matt?"

Taylor replied, "If that's a fancy word for lunatic, I ain't
in position to argue with you, Doc. But the more I study on
this job, the more it seems to me that being a mite crazy
helps. I don't mean mad-dog crazy like Clay Allison or that
Holliday gent who died over in the Colorado foothills of
consumption in the end. I was afraid Big Bill might be like
that when first we met. But now I think he's, well, *good* and
crazy, see?"

She laughed and said, "I do not. I've yet to see such a
mental condition described in any of the standard texts.
How can one say being crazy can be *good*?"

He said, "There you go trying to mix me up with all them
big words again, Doc. I never said it was good for Big Bill
to be a mite touched in the head. I meant it was good for
decent folk like yourself that Big Bill was crazy enough to
fight for you all, against odds, for what he's paid. A town
law that was too sane to take on the whole infernal Circle
Bar outfit would be as bad or worse than the homicidal
lunatic you seem to feel Big Bill is. I think he balanced
common sense and crazy bravery just about right so far. In

case he hasn't, would you mind going on the rest of the way alone, ma'am? I know it ain't decent, and I'm sure sorry. But I just got to get back there on the double, hear?"

She stopped, swung around to face him, and said flatly, "I don't want you going back there, Matt." Then she dropped her bag, reached up to wrap both arms around him, and kissed him flush on the lips.

He kissed back just as warmly—any man would have—but then he gently disengaged, and since he had no idea what he was supposed to say to her, he turned on one heel and headed back for the town lockup as, behind him, she stamped her foot on the plank walk and called out, "Come back here, you damned fool!"

But he never. He suspected that getting kissed so fine more than once would just ruin his resolve entire. It felt bad enough walking straight into who knew what, even without her warm kiss still tingling on his lips.

He barely made it back to the lockup in time. As he approached the front door one way, he spotted a line of torches up the street from the opposite direction, curb to curb and coming fast. He ran the last few yards and, as he entered, told the others laconically. "We're fixing to have company. Somebody help me slide the desk against the door."

But Big Bill shook his head and said, "You don't fort up in a packing crate, Matt. Break out one of the scatterguns and try to look mean as we discuss the matter with the Circle Bar. You other boys stay put at the windows, hear?"

Then Big Bill opened the door again and stepped out onto the front steps, Buntline Special in hand. Taylor blinked, gave a fatalistic shrug, and swiftly moved to the gun rack on one wall to procure and load a double-barrel ten-gauge. As he carried it port arms to the open doorway, he could see, past the bulk of Big Bill, that at least two dozen men, dressed cow and waving either torches or long guns of their own around, had lined up on the far side of the lantern-hung hitching rail in ominous silence.

Big Bill said nothing for what seemed an awkward hour, at the least, to Matt Taylor. Then a voice in the crowd called out, "We don't want to hurt nobody we don't have to, Marshal."

Big Bill called back, "That sounds reasonable. I suggest you boys go back to camp and get some sleep so's you can get your herd moving out in the dewsome cool of sunup."

The same voice called back, "We'd surely like to get us an early start, Marshal. But the Circle Bar looks after its own, if you follow my drift."

Big Bill chuckled understandingly and replied, "You can have the Mex for the asking, over to the wagon wright's, if you hurry. The town can't bury Robles afore his box is ready, it wouldn't be decent."

There was an angry rumble from the Circle Bar riders. The one who seemed to be the leader shushed them and called back, "What's done is done and what's fair is fair, Marshal. We heard about the fool kids picking a fight with you. So we're willing to forget about old Pablo eating the dust if you'll just be good enough to send Ben Fuller out to us. You have my word he'll ride on with us at sunup. Fair enough?"

Big Bill shook his head and said, "Not hardly. To begin with, I don't know whose word I'd be taking."

So the voice from the mob answered, "You're talking to Brazo Travis, the trail boss of the Circle Bar, and I ain't used to having folk doubt my word, hear?"

Big Bill chuckled again and called back, "I figured it was you. I just wanted to be sure. Nobody here doubts your good intent, Brazo, but try to see it our way. The boy ain't in condition to walk, let alone ride, even if he wasn't facing trial when and if he's up and around again."

The trail boss snapped, "We ain't here to see things your

way. We're here to make you see things *our* way, goddamn your eyes!"

Big Bill shook his head wearily and answered, "I ain't the one with eye trouble here. Suppose I let you see, with your own fool eyes, how just plain dumb you're talking? Would you like to come in, alone, for a look-see at young Fuller?"

There was a moment of hesitation. Then Brazo called back, "No tricks?" and it was Big Bill's turn to sound sullen as he answered, "I don't like to be called a liar, neither. We'll be proud to let you pay a bedside call on the little bastard on your one and only. If you're afraid, suit yourself."

Brazo cursed and stepped clear of the mob to reveal himself as an imposing hulk wearing gun-barrel chaps, a tall tan Stetson, and a brace of six-guns in a buscadero rig. As he circled the lit-up hitching rail, he kept his hands polite but called out, "I'd like to keep my hardware handy if it's all the same with you, Marshal." To which Big Bill replied in a jovial tone, "Suit your ferocious self, Brazo. I'll let you know if and when I start to worry about your guns. Nice rig. I'll bet you bought it in El Paso, right?"

As the burly Brazo came up the steps, he smiled despite himself and said, "Wrong. Had it made for me special in San Antone."

Big Bill said grudgingly, "I'll bet the saddler was a Mex, just the same. Nobody works leather that pretty, save a Mex."

As he joined them, Brazo grudgingly agreed, "All right, I had an old Mex carve the leather for me special in San Antone. But I never come here tonight to discuss my infernal gun rig. I'd like to see Ben Fuller now."

Big Bill ushered the trail boss inside, telling Tim Hogan to leave the door open lest the boys outside mistake his good intentions, but to shoot any son of a bitch who got within ten yards of the opening. Then, with Taylor and the ten-gauge tagging along, the marshal led Brazo back to the cell block. On the far side of the bars the wounded youth, bare to the waist save for the tape covering his wound and holding his right arm firmly against his chest, was semiconscious and cursing a blue streak in a groggy monotone. Brazo stared soberly through the bars at him for a time. Then he shrugged and said, "He do look poorly. Unlock this door so's I can visit him right."

Big Bill shook his head and said, "Not hardly. I ain't got the key ring handy."

The trail boss shot a confused look up at the taller man and demanded, "How come? Seems to me you'd *want* to keep your keys handy. I know *I* would if I was running a damned old jail."

Big Bill said, "Not if you was worried about a mob coming to lynch or free a prisoner, Brazo. The first thing I do at such unfriendly times is to hide the key ring so's I'm the only one as knows where it is. I didn't even tell my deputies where I hid it. Ain't that right, Matt?"

Taylor answered truthfully, "This is the first I've heard about the keys being hid, boss." So Big Bill smiled down at the confused trail boss to explain, "If anything happens to me, Lord knows how even my own boys could get your boy outten that there patent cell. Do you know what is a patent cell, Brazo?"

The trail boss had to admit he wasn't up on such matters. So Big Bill clinked the long barrel of his special against a bar and began with, "These bars is vanadium steel. It would take hours to cut through even one with a damned good hacksaw. You see, as you no doubt noticed, the building itself is just jerry-built of dry, splintersome wood. A prisoner could no doubt carve his way out with a belt buckle if he was really ambitious, and of course we can't have 'em setting fire to the floor, and they'll always get hold of

tobacco and matches even if we forbid it. So we sent away
to Pittsburgh for these here patent cells. They're called that
because they're patented by the steel company as makes
'em for small-town lockups all across the country. They
ship 'em in sections, and when you takes them outten the
crates you have to bolt 'em together, as you can see. Steel
walls, steel floor, steel ceiling, and naturally, all these bars
at one end. Ain't they just neat?"

Brazo stared uncertainly into the slate-gray interior and
conceded, "I can see you got the kid in a stout steel box.
How do we go about getting him *out*?"

Big Bill said flatly, "You don't. You and your boys might
take this frame shack by killing me and my boys, albeit I
wouldn't bet on that, but then where would you be? Fuller
would still be locked in that patent cell, and you and your
boys would be facing more serious charges than *he* is."

"Goddamn it, Marshal—" Brazo began.

But Big Bill cut him off to elaborate, "Your job is to get
the Circle Bar herd to the rail yards up Ogallala way, not to
wind up with reward posters out on you and all your hands.
I know how you feel responsible for this fool kid as well. In
your place I'd feel the same. But a man just has to get up
from the table when he sees he's throwing good money after
bad, right?"

Brazo said stubbornly, "We ain't talking money, damn it.
We're talking about a Texas boy entrusted to my care, and
I'm a mighty caring man."

Big Bill soothed, "Sure you are. That's why you ain't
going to get any of your *other* boys gut-shot or branded as
outlaws for the rest of their lives. How's it going to look if
you have to tell the owners of all that beef that you failed to
deliver one damn head because you was too busy commit-
ting murder and arson?"

Brazo blinked and asked, "Arson? How the hell did
arson get into this dumb conversation, Marshal?" only to

hear Big Bill reply cheerfully, "Oh, you ain't never going to get through me and my backup without a firefight, and this old lockup is a natural tinderbox. Of course, should a muzzle blast or a shot-up lamp set the building on fire, these patent cells back here can't burn. Young Fuller in there would likely just *bake*, sort of slow, no matter what you and your crew did to save him."

Brazo gulped and said, "Jesus, Marshal, you wouldn't let a thing like that happen on *purpose*, would you?"

Big Bill shrugged and said, "It do sound sort of cruel and unusual punishment for no more than an attempt charge. On the other hand, who's to say what a man going under with a mess of bullets in him might or might not feel like doing? Even the old Mex Rurales allow a dying man a last *smoke*, right?"

Brazo laughed weakly and said, "I think you're bluffing. I wish I knew for sure."

So Big Bill patted him on the shoulder to reply in a cheerful tone, "You don't. That's why you're just going to take your boys and your herd outten my town afore we have any more trouble with your outfit. It's been nice meeting you, Mr. Travis. But I can see you're anxious to get your herd on up the trail. So *adios*, you son of a bitch, and behave yourselves the next time you pass through my town, hear?"

The Circle Bar moved out just before sunrise, too subdued to even bust windows as they drove the herd through the slot between Freewater proper and the shanty-town–cum–red-light district on the Kansas side of the trail. Once they were gone, Big Bill Burton sent Matt Taylor and Tim Hogan home to get some shut-eye, since they'd have to pull the night shift until they could get rid of such a serious prisoner. He said he and Joe Walsh felt just fine for now, whether Joe had anything to say about it or not.

Taylor trudged home to his boardinghouse on the north side of Main Street just in time to miss breakfast. The elderly widow woman who ran the place shot him a severe look but said he might go back to the kitchen and ask her colored cook to fry him some eggs, at least. He declined with a weary smile, explained he'd had a hard night, and went on up to his little dormer room to shuck his duds and flop facedown across the iron cot, naked atop the covers. For now that it seemed over, he was feeling for the first time how tensed up he'd been most of the night.

But despite the season, by midafternoon the prairie sun beating on the slanting roof just above him had turned Taylor's room to a dry kiln more suited to seasoning lumber than to even trying to sleep. So he got up, hungry as a bitch wolf, had a quick bath and a shave, and went downstairs to discover it was pushing 4:00 P.M. Too early to report for duty and too late to start anything serious.

He dropped by the Prairie Dog for some chili con carne and pickled pig's feet, washed down with a schooner of draft, and then, seeing he still had some time on his hands, ambled over to the town library across from the schoolhouse. It wasn't much cooler inside. Autumn could be mighty sneaky on the High Plains. Miss Larsen, the librarian, still managed to look sort of icy under her stiffly starched mutton-sleeve blouse, buttoned up to her chin. The pretty but mighty prim ash-blonde stared back at him as he approached her desk in a manner suggesting the kids she taught earlier in the day behaved themselves indeed if they knew what was good for them. But she was sport enough to favor him with a frosty smile when he doffed his Stetson and asked how one went about borrowing books off the town.

She said, "To begin with, you need a library card. But since we all know you, Deputy Taylor, why don't you just go on back to the racks and select what you want as I make out a card for you."

He smiled at her, said that sounded more than fair, and did as he was told, feeling as if he'd somehow wound up back in school again. It was small wonder they said she was still unspoken for.

Back among all the dusty books, he had to browse around some before he found a couple of adventure books with lots of nice pictures in them. Then he wandered into an open space where more books lay along a big oak table. He didn't see exactly what he wanted. But he picked up a big, thick dictionary and took that back to the desk with him. As he put the modest pile down between them, Miss Larsen neither frowned nor smiled as she told him in her naturally snooty way, "I'm afraid we can't lend out any of our reference books, Deputy." And he was saved from asking a dumb question when she put the dictionary to one side and began to write the titles of the other books on his card, murmuring, "These look interesting. How old is the boy, sir?"

He blinked and said, "I ain't married up, ma'am. I was aiming to read these myself." And, to her credit, she just nodded and said, "Oh," in a tone that was neither mocking nor cover-up polite.

He cleared his throat and confided, "That's how come I wanted to borrow the dictionary, ma'am. You see, I *started* school, down home, but then my dad got crippled up by a rogue cow, and, well, me being the eldest and my ma having lots of more useless young-uns to feed, I just couldn't run the spread and go to school at the same time."

Her face didn't thaw, but her wide-set gray ices seemed mayhaps warm enough for trout to swim in as she said, "Well, if you really need this Webster's, I suppose we can lend out this one copy. You would have dropped out in about the fourth grade. Am I right?"

He smiled sheepishly across the desk at her and said, "Right on the money. How did you know, ma'am?"

She said, "I'm a schoolteacher. The boy's adventure books you chose were at that grade level. Wouldn't that have made you a bit young to run a cattle spread, sir?"

"Aw, I ain't no sir. My friends call me Matt. I was sort of big for my age at nine. I'd been riding and roping since I was a heap younger. I wouldn't want you spiting my folk for my being so dumb, though. Ma raised a real fuss about my staying home from school and said she was sure they could manage. My pa backed her, too. But what sort of a son would let his poor old busted-up father work that hard alone?"

She nodded understandingly but asked, "Couldn't your parents have hired at least a little help?"

So Taylor sighed and told her, "Not at first, betwixt the doctor bills and the price of beef that year. By the time I was twelve or so we had things humming better and Dad did take on an old breed who wasn't bad at roping. But by then I was roping even better, and what kind of a fool would I have looked, going back to the fourth grade as old as I'd got by then?"

She sighed wearily and said, "You don't have to explain, ah, Matt. I've been teaching school in cattle country awhile. But as long as you're taking Webster's home with you, would you mind if I make a suggestion?"

He said he didn't. So she left him there and went back to the stacks herself. She knew right where to go. She was back in no time with a couple of awesomely thick books. She put them down and moved back around to her side of the desk again before she told him, "These are the same sort of stories you selected. But they were written for somewhat older boys, see?"

He peered down at the Malory she'd picked out for him and read aloud, *"King Arthur and his . . . Knots?"*

She said, "Knights. The same as in this children's book, but perhaps more suited to a grown man's taste. You may find that dictionary handy, wading through Malory. This *Robinson Crusoe* ought to be easier sledding for you, even though it's considered an adult novel. Are you game, cowboy?"

He laughed and said, "Sure. It ain't like a book's likely to roll on you, even if it bucks you off. But can I have the kid books, too? You see, I may have a lot of time to read for the next few nights. I'm pulling night watch on a felony prisoner."

She nodded soberly and said, "I heard about that. Everyone in town was holding his or her breath until that herd left this morning. Are you going to hang the one who survived?"

He said, "It ain't up to me to say. To tell the truth, that was the book I really wanted. But I can see you ain't got it. So your guess is as good as mine."

She naturally asked what book he was talking about and looked downright startled when he said, "Law book. I was hoping you'd have a book with the state laws of Colorado handy."

She smiled incredulously and asked, "Did you really think all the statutes of even one state would be in one book? Good heavens, you're talking about a whole rack of criminal law before you even get to civil statutes." Then she looked away from him as she added in a softer tone, "I'm not sure you'd be ready for legal tomes if we stocked them, Matt. Some of the Latin terms are above *my* head and, well . . ."

"I follow your drift," he cut in, adding, "This sure is vexicating, though. You need more common sense than book learning, working with cows. But anyone can see a lawman ought to know the law, and, well, to tell the pure truth, I ain't sure I'm up to King Arthur and his nights."

She didn't look frosty at all as she told him, "I'll go through the catalogs this evening and see what I can do. There may be a basic law primer. If there isn't, there certainly ought to be. Why don't we talk about it when you bring those books back?"

He agreed and put his hat back on to scoop them up. As he thanked her and turned to go, she hesitated, then called his back, saying, "I can see that, educated or not, you're interested in justice. I'm having a problem with one of my students."

He grinned crookedly and asked, "You want me to arrest a bitty kid for you, Miss Larsen?"

She shook her head and said, "Call me Inga. That's what my friends call me. I don't want poor little Tommy Hatfield put in jail. But *somebody* should be. He keeps coming to school all black and blue. I haven't been able to get him to tell me who's been abusing him at home. But somebody certainly must be!"

He nodded soberly and said, "It don't take a law degree to see *that* can't be right. I'll have a word about it with my boss. You say the kid's folk are called Hatfield, Miss Inga?"

She nodded and said, "Yes, they're homesteaders, a mile or so northeast of town. I'm worried about the boy walking all that way to school once winter sets in, too. They dress him thin, and if he has a pair of shoes to his name, I've yet to see them."

He said he got the picture, and left. When he got to the lockup he discovered Tim Hogan had already reported in, so Joe had left, mighty sleepy, according to Tim. Big Bill, seated at his desk, yawned and got to his feet, saying, "She's all your'n, old son. What you got there?"

Taylor put his load down on the desk, saying, "Books. By the way, do we have any law books around here, boss?"

Big Bill tapped the side of his head as he replied, "I got all I need to know right here. Judge Carver has all the books he may need to nitpick. That ain't our problem. Anyone with common sense can haul a sinner before the judge, and after that, it's up to *him* to decide whether to let the bastard off or not. Are you mixed up about some sinner, old son?"

Taylor told him about the teacher's concern for one of her students, or tried to, before Big Bill cut him off with, "I know about the Hatfields. They're trash-white nesters trying to grow truck in a land the good Lord made for cows. Their claim is on the far side of the Kansas line. There ain't much we can do about the way old Jeff Hatfield treats his wife and kids when he's been at the jar. I've told him more than once that it's dangerous for even a trash white to drink white lightning meant for Indians. But like I said, he votes in Kansas, if he votes at all."

Taylor frowned and said, "His kid goes to school here in Freewater. Don't that give us some jurisdiction, boss?"

The town law shrugged and said, "Sure it does, if the little bastard steals so much as an apple here in town. If you ever see his dear old drunken daddy beating him, serious, on the streets of Freewater, feel free to haul him in as well. The Hatfield homestead and anything as goes on there is for *Kansas* to worry about, see?"

Taylor shook his head and said, "Hold on. You said any peace officer has the duty to stop any crime in progress he sees going on in any jurisdiction, and the nearest Kansas lawman is a day's ride from here, remember?"

Big Bill yawned again and said, "Sure I do. So I'll tell you what. If it worries you so much, just ride over there and kill the damned old drunk. Nobody in Kansas is likely to mind, and do you haul him afore Judge Carver, the old fart will just rawhide you and turn Hatfield loose."

Taylor grimaced and said, "I can't see shooting down a man in cold blood, whether he's drunk or sober."

Big Bill nodded and said, "That's why I've never done it. I've had more than one complaint about that worthless son of a bitch. But there's nothing we can do about him but hope he drinks his fool self to death or at least has the courtesy to beat up a grown man here in town. The bastard's too slick to show up in town drunk and disorderly. He saves all his bravery for his wife and kids."

He saw that Taylor still looked unconvinced. So he moved closer, put a fatherly paw on the younger man's shoulder, and said, "Look, Matt, if you're going to be a lawman, one of the first things you got to savvy is that no lawman with a lick of sense mixes up in *family* matters. Do you get betwixt man and wife in a free-for-all, you're more likely to get hurt then *they* are. Sometimes I suspicion half the women getting beat up by men must be crazy gals who asked for it. For no sooner does a helpsome lawman step betwixt a woman and a wife beater than she's stabbing him with a hat pin or worse. Lawmen have been killed mixing up in family fights, and even when you do manage to haul the brute before a judge, his infernal victim refuses to press charges nine times outten ten, see?"

Taylor nodded wearily but said, "It still seems a shame we can't help the kid, though." To which Big Bill replied, with a knowing grin, "Don't you mean his schoolmarm, that Miss Larsen? I think she's mighty handsome, too. But even if you could, would you really want to wind up with frostbite down there?"

Taylor scowled and said, "Hold on! I never told the gal I'd see what I could do because I was out to mess with her!"

Big Bill said, "Good. I'm too sleepy right now to worry about you romantic little rascals." And then he left, chuckling to himself.

From where he was seated on an ammo case in one corner, Tim Hogan laughed and asked Taylor, "What'll you bet he's on his way to Freewater Fannie's to get romantical as hell? I hear tell he gets it free over there, from the madam herself."

Taylor sat down at the desk, growling, "I don't know why every damn fool around here wants to talk dirty today. This is supposed to be the town lockup, not a cathouse, damn it."

Tim shrugged and said, "Mayhaps you've been getting more than the rest of us, Matt. 'Fess up; I know you must have some gal in town by now. The only gents who don't talk horny are the ones who get it regular. I don't suppose your gal would like to fix me up with a friend? I been in town a lot longer than you, and save for them mighty expensive fancy gals down to the east end, I just ain't been able to find me a willing she-male in this town, even an ugly one."

Taylor chuckled and said, "Hell, Tim, that ain't no mystery. There just ain't no gal in this town ugly enough to want you. I got some books here I'd sure like to read, if you're through talking like a kid."

"You got *somebody*." Tim insisted sullenly, adding, "I can tell. You can't fool me."

Taylor tipped his hat back, picked up the King Arthur book, and made himself comfortable in Big Bill's chair to see if he could wrangle it.

He could, but only with the help of the dictionary Miss Inga had been nice enough to lend him against the rules. That made him sort of wonder about other rules she might or might not be willing to break, despite her prim and proper ways. Wouldn't it be something to see all that ash-blond hair down, over all that cool flesh a gal would just have to have not to sweat on such a sultry day, all buttoned up in that thin starched blouse that didn't really hide all that much to a man with any imagination?

He found himself reading the same line twice, and it hadn't been about any old gal, either time. So why in thunder should he be thinking of old Icy Inga when, hell, the only gal in town he'd ever kissed was the doc and . . .

"Damn you to hell, Tim Hogan!" he declared, closing the book with a snap.

Hogan stared owlishly at him to protest, "What did I do now, Matt? I ain't said word one since you started reading that fool book."

Taylor growled, "I know. But this infernal long-winded tale is about riders in tin suits having knife fights on horseback, and thanks to you, I can't keep my mind on such goings-on right now."

Tim shrugged and asked, "What do you reckon we ought to talk about, then?"

To which Taylor replied with a sigh, "Nothing. If you been here all this time without meeting any halfway decent gals, there ain't a thing you could tell me that would help all that much. Mayhaps I'll try this other book, about Bob Crusoe. He sure dressed funny, judging by the picture. I wonder how come, or if there's any tips on meeting up with frisky gals in *this* one. Being a night in a tin suit sounds tedious as herding cows, to tell the truth."

By the time Taylor had served out the time he'd agreed to, Big Bill had made no apparent effort to find another deputy, and neither of them saw fit to mention the matter. Taylor still had his doubts about his own ability or desire to cut it as a lawman. But every time he gave serious thought to seeking another job, he had to admit there were compensations to the one he had.

The glory days of the cowboy had been the big beef boom between, say, 1880 to the grim winter of 1887–88. The financial panic and depression of the 1870s had ended with prosperity and a great demand for fresh beef in the East, delivered from the packing plants of Omaha, Chicago, et al., via the newfangled refrigerated boxcar, actually a glorified icebox on wheels. This in turn had occasioned monstrous expansion of the cattle industry, with big business corporations, many international in scope, carving vast cattle empires out of the still thinly populated western states and territories. So for one all too short golden age, the original Tex-Mex vaquero or buckaroo, trained in the arts of managing half-wild cattle on unfenced and rugged open range, had been able to write his own ticket, while almost any man or boy who could stay aboard a horse or mule had been welcomed as a cowhand until he'd had enough and quit, been crippled or killed, or learned the required skills. But that great expansion of the eighties had been followed by the inevitable red ink on the books occasioned by just too many damned cows to sustain the inflated beef prices, coupled with the inevitable losses many a cattle company suffered on marginal range or due to poor management by absentee ownership. Some of the biggest herds had been owned, for a short time, by investors in London or Glasgow who'd never seen a longhorn on the hoof, let alone the poor range they'd leased or the ragtag collections of misfits they'd hired at long distance to mistreat both the herds and range. So after the huge losses of the big freeze of 1887–88 had wiped out whole herds from the Canadian border to south Texas, the quick-money boys had not only pulled out but left a small army of fair cowhands adrift and unemployed.

There were still jobs to be had, of course. Folk still liked steak and potatoes in the ever-expanding industrial East. But the outfits left, the outfits run by hard-nosed businessmen who knew what they were doing, were in a position to pick and choose their hired help, and did. They expected top-hand skills from every rider. So gone were the days when a real buckaroo could refuse such unmanly chores as stringing fences or whitewashing the barn.

Taylor knew that any new outfit he joined would call him the new kid and expect him to help the cook when asked, until such time as an even greener hand was hired. For it was "Last hired, first fired" in an industry that now guarded seniority with the same desperation as the trade unions in more settled parts.

He knew he could still *get* a job working cows, and likely as a top hand, because he was better than most at such work. But on the other hand, despite his misgivings, he found himself accepted as a lawman by both his peers and the townsfolk as well, after less than two weeks of arrival in Freewater. He knew no cow outfit would refer to him as anything but the new kid for at least eight weeks and a fight in town with another outfit, provided he distinguished himself in battle.

Of course, fistfights between likkered-up outfits seldom resulted in death or serious injury. So it seemed natural the folk in Freewater treated him so respectful after he'd mixed in two shoot-outs on their behalf. It still felt good, though. And, what the hell, it was too late in the year to sign on for anyone's fall roundup, and riding winter range as the new kid sounded sort of grim. So he hadn't gotten around to telling Big Bill he was quitting just yet. He sort of stayed on.

As the last trail herds of the season moved through without too much trouble, things got so quiet in Freewater that he almost felt guilty about his position. The night duty was galling, even with books to read, and as the wounded Ben Fuller recovered from his first meek weakness, he took to saying things about Taylor's poor dead mother that called for professional restraint indeed on Taylor's part. One night Tim Hogan wanted to go back and beat some decency into the nasty little cuss, but Taylor told him not to, and Tim seemed to accept that as an order from a superior.

Taylor still felt more confused than superior. Helen Harris still came by once a day to have a look at Fuller's wound and a couple of times to lance it, according to the day shift. But she never came by in the evenings when Taylor was on duty, and the one time he passed her on the street, she just looked right through him and kept walking as he stood there like a fool with his hat off.

Women were surely a caution to figure. For no reason he could see, the lady doc who'd seemed so warm-natured at first was the one who acted so cold, once she'd teased a man to where he gave a hang, whereas Miss Inga, who looked as if she could freeze a man in his boots, until you got to know her, was starting to smile downright human at him every time he swapped books with her at the library.

She'd been a good sport when he'd told her what Big Bill had said about the Hatfield family. She'd even thanked him for his trying. She'd found him a schoolbook, a high school book, on what they called "civics." It wasn't a real law book. But at least it explained more than he'd ever even wondered about how towns were run. It told how a state was made up of counties and how a county was made up of townships and just what the different governments of each were supposed to worry about the most. It even had the whole text of the U.S. Constitution in the back of the book. He really needed the dictionary to wade through *that* chore. He was surprised to learn that what he'd always thought to be the Constitution was only the Bill of Rights they'd tacked on it at the end. The whole thing was filled with thunder-gasting fancy words, as well as too damned long to grasp in one reading. He had to go over it three or four times before he began to make some sense of it. He admired that balance of power notion. He'd always thought the law could do most anything to you if you messed with it.

He failed to see why it made Miss Inga all dewy-eyed when he renewed his loan on her civics book and explained why he wanted to get it all down pat in his dumb head. She said soberly, "I don't think you could be very dumb, Matt. Do you know I have you reading at high-school level now?"

He started to ask what she was talking about. But mayhaps because he'd been reading the books she'd suggested for his night reading, he just grinned at her and said, "You're sure sneaky, no offense. I never would have picked out that swell yarn about the two cities on my own, and I doubt I'd have finished that long-winded tale of Ivanhoe if I hadn't suspected you'd ask questions. I thought that fool book would never get to the point."

She dimpled at him and confided, "A lot of people find Sir Walter Scott rough going. I'm proud of you for finishing *Ivanhoe*. How did you like the story itself?"

He shrugged and said, "I surely could have told it in a lot fewer words. I figured out why you thought a lawman ought to read it, by the end. Ivanhoe was a natural lawman who just done what was right. That poor Templar got so torn up betwixt sworn duty and his own feelings that it killed him in the end. I'd have married up with that Jew gal who done so much for me if I'd been old Ivanhoe, though. She was the only gal in the book with a lick of spunk. She kept helping him and helping him, and in the end he run off with that sappy Saxon princess who never raised a finger for nobody, as far as I could see. Don't you think Ivanhoe acted a mite ungrateful as well as dumb?"

She stared wide-eyed at him and said, "I can't believe it. Do you know that was the theme of my college thesis on Walter Scott?"

He shrugged and said, "I'm sure you used bigger words. But it don't take a college education to see old Scott was a sort of long-winded snob who put more store in fancy breeding than whether folk act decent or not."

She smiled so warmly at him, he wondered how on earth he could have ever taken her for a cold and snooty lass as she said, "I've got another book I want you to read, Matt."

He said he was game. So she ran back to the stacks and broke out a copy of the *Iliad*, by Homer. It was illustrated.

So he was able to say, "I dunno, Miss Inga. These old boys sure look odd running about half-naked in firemen's helmets. What's it about?"

She said, "What you were talking about before. The conflict between duty and desire. It's the first great tragedy of our western civilization. But no author has ever improved on Homer when it comes to dealing with the dreadful results when duty and desire, or even duty and common sense, lead down two different roads."

He said, "Well, these old boys sure don't look like any western folk I've ever met. But you ain't steered me wrong yet."

So she put him down on his card for Homer as well while he shot a wistful look at the Regulator clock on the wall above her and said, "I'd best get on over to the lockup. I was wondering, though . . ." To which she answered quietly, "Yes?" And he said, "I was wondering how come you're out to educate me so much. Is it because ignorant lawmen make you nervous or is it because you're just a born teacher, Miss Inga?"

She looked away from him and murmured, "Maybe it's a little of both." Then, when he nodded and gave her an *adios* for now, she flounced back to the stacks and commenced slamming books all about for some fool reason. Women sure were odd little critters.

When he got to the lockup he was surprised to find Helen as well as Big Bill arguing in the front office. He put his books on an ammo case and joined the lady doc near Big Bill's desk. She shot Taylor a curt nod and went right back to fussing at the seated marshal, saying, "He's not up to a horseback ride like that in his condition, damn it!"

Big Bill chuckled fondly and said, "Neither am I, little lady. I mean to drive us over to the county seat by buckboard."

She insisted, "I'm not sure that infection has cleared up

yet. Can't it at least wait until morning? The nights are cold this late in the season, Marshal."

Big Bill shrugged and replied, "They'll be getting colder before they get any warmer, ma'am. I want to get him over there before the circuit judge leaves again, and you're fussing at the wrong cuss. It was Judge Carver, not me, who decided the charge requires a county trial. I don't see why, neither."

Taylor said, "I do. Judge Carver's only empowered to hold a magistrate's court. To put Fuller in state prison you need to charge him before a county judge and jury, boss."

Big Bill stared up at him blankly to reply, "Says who?"

So Taylor said, "The U.S. Constitution and likely the state one. I ain't read the Colorado constitution yet, but it can't be that far off. The accused has the right to a jury trail in all cases involving a serious felony or a suit for more than twenty dollars, unless he or she is willing to face a lower court."

Big Bill's jaw dropped. He recovered enough to say, "Jesus H. Christ. Sorry, ma'am. What's got into you, Matt? You sound as nitpicky about the law as Judge Carver all of a sudden!"

Taylor shrugged modestly and allowed, "I've been reading me some books. But it's for Judge Carver to say, of course. He could likely let Fuller off with a fine and the time already served without a jury trial. I doubt Fuller would object."

Big Bill said, "Don't tempt me. If he was at all repentsome, I might feel he'd larnt his lesson. But every time we feed him he says mean things and brags on killing me the minute he gets out. So I mean to see he serves some serious time, and that's about the size of it."

Helen protested, "He's as likely to die if he catches a chill riding all that way on an open buckboard with the north wind blowing dark."

Big Bill shrugged and insisted as stubbornly, "I'll give him a blanket to wrap up in, and if he dies, he dies. It was his notion, not mine, to engage in armed conflict. Had I known how much extra trouble it was going to cost me, I'd have never took him alive to begin with." Then he nodded at Taylor to add, "You'd best see Miss Helen home now, Matt. We won't be needing two men on duty tonight. Soon as Tim shows up, I'll be carrying Fuller over to the county seat, hear?"

He sounded like he meant it. Taylor took Helen's elbow in hand to suggest they leave. She shrugged him off and snapped, "I can get home as safe or safer by myself, thank you very much!"

Then she flounced out, slamming the door behind her. Big Bill winked up at Taylor and said, "Go after her, old son. Can't you see she fancies you?"

Taylor frowned and answered, "Do tell? She sure don't act like it."

To which his older mentor replied knowingly, "Gals are like that. I don't know why, neither. I ain't a gal. But take it from me, she's got the hots for you, you lucky devil."

Taylor snorted in disbelief and asked, "Are you saying you can tell a gal likes you when she's acting spitesome? What would that make a gal who *smiled* at you a lot, then?"

Big Bill shrugged and said, "A flirt. Gals like to practice on gents they don't really care about. You see, the poor little things are in control of themselves when a gent don't matter to 'em. But once they get really hot for a man, it drives 'em sort of *loco en la cabeza*. I know this to be true because one of the sweetest-loving little gals I ever had commenced our relationship by stabbing me. Not serious enough to matter, of course. When a woman really kills a man, it's safe to assume she was really sore at him. The doc ain't even stuck you with a hat pin, so what are you waiting for, you fool?"

Taylor laughed, picked up his books, and headed for the door. But as he was leaving, Big Bill called him back to say, "I almost forgot. I may be over to the county seat a few days, bearing witness against that Fuller boy. I want you to be in charge while I'm gone, savvy?"

Taylor protested, "Tim and Joe both have seniority, don't they?"

But Big Bill insisted, "They won't argue about it with you. How many bank robberies have either of 'em ever stopped? You got good sense as well as more hair on your chest, Matt. I doubt any more trouble is headed this way ahead of the first snow. But I'll feel better knowing you're running things here if anything serious should come up."

Taylor shrugged, allowed Big Bill was the boss, and went on out. It was still light outside, and since he knew where Helen lived, he could have caught up with her had he tried, but she'd already made a fool of him on the streets of Freewater, so he didn't try. He went home, just in time to be served a warmed-over supper and a scolding from the widow woman, and then, since it was too early for bed, carried his books into the parlor to read. He found the *Ilaid* rough going indeed. For it was put together like poetry that didn't rhyme, and everyone had sort of funny names. He might have done better had he known why in thunder that pretty blond library gal had wanted him to read it. If Big Bill was at all right about women, Miss Inga was just funning with him, and the doc was just as pretty. He wondered what might happen if he just went over to the clinic and asked her right out for another kiss. But if Big Bill was wrong, he'd no doubt get his fool head bashed in. So he stuck it out until old Homer began to make more sense than any fool *she-male* around there.

He made breakfast, easy, the next morning, and ambled over to the lockup to turn Tim loose and see if there was

anything else going on. Tim got up from behind the desk
and handed him a note from Big Bill, asking him to pay a
call on the city council at 10:00 A.M. The note didn't say
why. Taylor put it aside as he took the vacant seat,
muttering, "Funny he never mentioned it last night. They'd
have all gone home by that time. So they must have asked
him earlier. Mayhaps he just forgot."

Tim stretched, hitched his belt, and headed for the door
with a noncommittal comment. Then he turned to say, "I
know what's up. You promise not to say I talked to you
about it?"

Taylor nodded. So Tim explained, "Big Bill's been trying
to put it off. He's on mighty friendly terms with some of the
gals at the east end of town. Between you and me, I'd say
that was his main reason for carrying Fuller over to the
county seat. I've seen him let many a wild young cuss leave
town with a boot in the ass and no guns worth mention."

Taylor leaned back in the chair and hooked one spurred
boot over a corner of the desk as he sighed and said, "I hope
you're wrong. I'd rather swamp stables than clean out
whorehousing, and I can see Burton's point. I can't see how
that end of town comes under our jurisdiction, being in
Kansas as it is."

Tim said, "Running the whores and tinhorns out entire
ain't exactly what the town council has in mind. They're
good for the more seemly businesses on this side of the
cattle trail. The town council wants to make 'em pay
business taxes, just like everyone else in town has to."

Taylor laughed and said, "Hell, Tim, they ain't really *in*
the township of Freewater. How can a Colorado city council
tax a cathouse in Kansas?"

Tim said, "Don't ask me. I just work here. Big Bill asked
'em the same question. They told him they had them a
special ruling from Judge Carver. They'll likely explain it

all to you at the ten o'clock meeting." Then he left to get some sleep.

But thanks to Tim's warning and the fretting Taylor got to do as he watched the hands of the wall clock creep around for a year or more, Taylor's mind was made up when he entered the town hall a few minutes early to face the council down.

Mayor Smiley, the fat banker, was presiding, of course. Matt Taylor knew most of the others at least by sight as he took his hardwood seat across the long table from them. The crusty old Judge Carver wasn't there. He'd likely read some law books in his time. The mayor said some nice things about Taylor before he got down to brass tacks, saying, "You doubtless know those riffraff at the east end of town have been enjoying a free ride at our expense, Deputy Taylor. They're the only folk in town who expect our civic services at no cost to themselves. We've agreed it's time they paid proper taxes, the same as all the other profit-making establishments in town."

An old goat down at the end of the table cackled and chimed in with, "Lord knows Freewater Fannie charges more for a piece of tail than I get for a shave and a haircut!" Which made the others laugh and inspired another to opine, "You ought to know, you horny rascal."

Mayor Smiley banged on the table for silence and said, "This is serious, damn it." Then he told Taylor, "We have the tax assessments all drawn up, Deputy. All you have to do is see that they're served on the wretched freeloaders, see?"

Taylor replied soberly, "Not hardly. I got some questions to ask first. To begin with, do them whores and worse at the east end get to vote on your town taxes or, for that matter, any of you gents as want to tax 'em?"

There was a growl of outraged disbelief before Mayor Smiley could shush them and snap, prim-lipped, "Of course not. Them women wouldn't have the vote, even if they was decent and living in Colorado. The pimps and gamblers may be allowed to vote in Kansas, of course. But not in Colorado. Didn't you know that red-light district was across the state line, son?"

Taylor nodded and said, "I sure thought it was. That's why I can't hardly serve no tax bills on anyone over yonder. That'd be taxation without representation. That can't be right."

As the rest of them stared at him, stunned, Mayor Smiley asked, "Sweet Jesus, son, are you sticking up for them disgusting honky-tonk whores and gamblers in defiance of law and order?"

Taylor replied, "Nope. As a lawman, it's the law I'm sworn to uphold. I'm empowered to go down to that end of town and bust up fights or other crimes in progress, provided that the state of Kansas don't tell me not to, and so far, they've never. I'm not sure about gambling, but I suspect prostitution may be a violation of Kansas law. If you want the east end cleaned out, I can wire the nearest Kansas sheriff and we may be able to run all that trash up the trail a piece, if that's what you want."

A saloon owner to Smiley's right asked, "Are you out of your mind, boy? How many herds would stop here in Freewater if they couldn't get laid, for God's sake?"

Taylor shrugged and said, "Not many, I reckon. So ain't them gals providing as much or more service to Freewater than vice versa? We don't even pick up their garbage, as far as I know. If I was you, I'd just live and let live until such time as you and the voters decide to issue whoring and gambling licenses. I'd be proud to see that nobody operated a whorehouse or gambling hell without a license, if one was required."

The burly smith who ran the smithy and livery just inside the bounds of decency, or the Ogallala Trail, snapped,

"Well, you ain't *us*, damn it! It's for this council to make the rules in this town, and it's for you to see that they're *obeyed*, see?"

Matt Taylor nodded, rose to his feet, and unpinned his brass badge as he said, "It's your town. This here is your badge. I never put it on to serve as a pimp for anybody. You owe me close to a month's wages, by the way. I'll let you work it out with Marshal Burton when he gets back. I'll leave a forwarding address with him as soon as I figure out where I'll be going."

Mayor Smiley, who had his bank to worry about as well, said, "Hold on now, damn it. You can't run off and leave us with no law here in Freewater, son."

Taylor said, "Sure I can. The U.S. Constitution says I can. You boys don't want a lawman, anyway. You want a bill collector to collect from folk who don't owe you all that much to begin with. I ain't about to shake down whores for money. You'll just have to find another boy."

Mayor Smiley said, "Oh, for God's sake, pin that star back on and behave yourself, Taylor. We can always talk about taxing them riffraff another time."

Taylor said, "Not with me." And then, hearing no objections, he pinned the badge back on and asked if they had any other orders for him. Mayor Smiley said they didn't. So he favored them all with a friendly smile and turned to leave. As he was going out the door he heard someone behind him mutter, "He sure is a touchy young cuss. Good lawman, though."

Taylor thought no more of the matter as the day wore on as quietly as only days in a sleepy trail town with no herds in sight can manage. With no prisoners in the back and with most of the citizenry knowing where to find him in an emergency, he ordered Joe to go home and told Tim Hogan to stay awake anywhere he wanted, as long as he didn't outright ignore gunshots in the wee small hours. Then he locked up, went home for supper, and, not feeling up to another session with library books, wandered over to the Prairie Dog for such cheer as they might have on tap.

They didn't have much. The place was nearly deserted. As he passed some time with Sean, the barkeep, a young tough whose black suit was pressed smoother than his scarred-up face came in to stand next to Taylor at the bar and murmur, "Madame Fannie would like a word with you, if you can spare the time, Deputy."

Taylor sighed and said, "Oh, hell, I ain't coming at her with any fool papers, if that's what she's worried about."

The pimp replied, "We heard. I think that's what she wants to talk to you about."

Taylor muttered about small-town gossip, finished his beer, and left with the fancy boy. It was a short enough walk. A long walk would take one clean through Freewater. He'd been to the notorious gal's house of ill repute before, the time he'd gone after Grat Lewis that first night in town. So he was surprised and not too reassured when his somewhat sinister guide led him up a cinder-paved lane in the unlit end of town to point at a cottage behind a picket fence and say, "In there, Deputy."

Taylor put a thoughtful hand on the grips of his .44–40 as he said, not unkindly, "You go first, *amigo*."

The pimp chuckled and took the lead. He knocked and then opened the door, calling out, "I got him, Miss Fannie. He thinks I'm trying to set him up."

A contralto voice inside laughed and asked them both to come in. Taylor still made the pimp go first. But he relaxed his guard once they were inside, staring down at a once lovely lady of about forty, give or take a hard life. Freewater Fannie was reclining on a red velvet sofa in a red silk kimono. Her hair and the pom-poms on her slippers were the same color. One got the impression she liked red. She waved her messenger boy back outside, referring to him as Marcel. When she saw the look on Taylor's face, she smiled wryly up at him and said, "My real name isn't Fannie, either. But everyone deserves to be called *something*. Sit down, handsome. Make yourself comfortable. Is there anything I can get you? A drink? A blow job?"

He removed his Stetson and found another seat to perch on. It looked something like an overgrown tomato on gilt legs. He said, "I ain't here as a customer, ma'am. Your, ah, Marcel, said you wanted to see me about something."

She nodded and said, "I owe you for what you did for me today. I wasn't invited to attend the meeting myself, but a girl has friends. So what's your price?"

He frowned at her and replied, "Price, ma'am? No offense, but I don't follow your drift at all."

She smiled knowingly at him and said, "Come on, don't be coy. I'm old enough to be your mother, if I wasn't so careful, and I've yet to have a man go out on a limb for me without I paid him back with love or money. It's been a while since I've had to pay off with my body, but to tell the truth, I might not mind with a young stud like you. But I suppose you'd rather talk finances, eh? Men as good-looking as you tend to be sort of cold to us working girls, seeing what they can get for free off the amateur talent in this competitive world."

He stared at her, bemused, and said, "Miss Fannie, I surely wish I knew what we were talking about. First you tell me that you're my mother, which hardly seems possible, and then you're talking about my romantical life, which hasn't been all that interesting, and as for finances, that was what the whole fuss with the city council was about. They said they wanted me to collect taxes off you and the other ladies in your line of work, and I said I wouldn't, and that was the end of it."

She stared at him for a moment of silence, as if she were

a gypsy gal staring into a teacup and wasn't able to read her fortune worth a hang. Finally she tried, "Let me see if I've got this straight. They ordered you to shake us down and you refused for no damned reason at all?"

He shook his head and said, "Of course I had a reason. I'm a peace officer, not a pimp, no offense. You're right in calling their notion a shakedown. That's all it would be. As far as I can see, you folk on this side of the trail ain't subject to the taxing powers of Freewater Township. I don't know why I can't seem to make anyone *else* see that. It's just common sense and simple justice, right?"

She swallowed and said, "My God, I think you're real. How on earth did a nice boy like you ever get into a joint like this? I mean Freewater, not here. You've got no more call to wear that badge than one of my whores. Less, in fact. They *know* the way the law works in these parts, you poor baby."

He shrugged and said, "I know I got a lot to learn. I've been reading all the books I can. It was your boyfriend, Big Bill, as hired me. I told him I knew more about cows than the law."

She wrinkled her nose and said, "I'll forget that remark about Bill Burton and me, since I know where you heard it. I don't supposed you'd believe me if I told you our friendship was more platonic than some say?"

He said, "Sure I believe you, ma'am. I never call nobody a liar until I catch 'em lying to me. What's betwixt you and Big Bill ain't none of my beeswax in any case, right?"

She made the sign of the cross and muttered, "Jesus, Mary, and Joseph, what's a nice little kid like you doing out on the street at this hour? Bill Burton should be ashamed of himself!"

He said, "Oh, I don't know, ma'am. I can handle myself in a fight when I have to."

She said, "We heard about you and the Redford brothers.

That's not the point. You're nothing but an honest young man, Matt Taylor!"

He asked her what was wrong with honesty in a lawman. So she told him, "That's not the way this world works, Matt. You're just going to die poor as well as young if you don't wise up. You're the first lawman I've met who wasn't a back-shooting four-flusher on the take! Can't you see Bill Burton stuck you with the showdown with the city council today?"

He shook his head and said, "Judge Carver was the one as told Big Bill he had to carry Fuller over to the county seat, ma'am. As for his being a back-shooter, I can't say he wouldn't, if he had the call to. But I was there when he shot it out face-to-face at two-to-one odds."

She laughed bitterly and said, "Far be it for me to cast doubt on his showboating with that fancy gun of his. I can see you think he's the bee's knees. If there's nothing I can do for you tonight, I'll just have to owe you, Matt Taylor. I know what you think of me. But there *was* a time I thought the world was run on the level. So meeting up with you has sort of restored my faith in men. Some men, anyway. Most of you seem to be hard-hearted he-goats."

He chuckled and replied, "I reckon the good Lord slipped up when he was working on old Adam's rib, ma'am. Men and women no doubt deserve something better than one another. But that's the way it is. You can't savvy us and we can't savvy you. Ain't that a bitch?"

She sighed and said, "There are times I wish I didn't understand men as well as I do. It's only the rare ones, like you, that mix me up worth mention. You feel insulted if I told you I liked you, Matt Taylor?"

He answered soberly, "No, ma'am. I think you're nice, too. But now that we've admired one another with all the cards on the table, I'd best get it on down the road if it's all the same with you."

She nodded, and as he rose, she rose with him. She was shorter, standing up, than he'd expected. She followed him to her door, and as he ticked his hat brim at her, she murmured, "God, if I was but twenty years younger. Look after yourself, Matt, and if there's anything you ever need . . . Oh, get out of here, you fool kid!"

As Taylor crossed the churned-up cattle trail to head on up Main Street, Tim Hogan ran up to him, saying, "I've been looking all over for you, Matt. You're wanted at the clinic. That Miss Larsen from the schoolhouse brung a sick kid to the lady doc and they've both been asking for you a heap!"

Taylor broke into a quick-march as he asked the deputy tagging along with him for more details. Hogan didn't have many. He said, "A nester gal brung him in by buckboard just a few mintues back. Looks to me like he got hay-bailed or something. I only got a glimpse of him as I was helping the teacher and the doc carry him inside. His mama carried him to the schoolhouse, not knowing where the clinic was. The schoolhouse was closed, of course, but the fool woman was raising such a fuss that Miss Larsen come out of her own quarters, across the schoolyard, and the two of 'em tore over to the clinic with him. Someone had already put a wool blanket over him. I asked what had happened, but they both yelled at me to fetch you. So I just did."

Taylor said, "You done right. You'd best get Walsh and open up the lockup. I'll meet you there as soon as I get to arrest somebody."

Then he started running. It wasn't all that far. But when he tore past the buckboard out front and into the waiting room, he found Inga Larsen glaring up at him as if it was all his fault, and about time he got there. Inga was seated on the waiting bench with a shabby-dressed gal, trying to comfort her. She looked as if she could use it. Her thin calico Mother Hubbard was torn, and her vapidly pretty but emaciated face was swollen on one side. He asked Inga what had happened. She just managed to blurt out, "This is Tommy Hatfield's mother," when Helen stuck her head out and called, "In here, Matt. I want you to see this before I put more dressings on."

He went into her treatment room. He took one look at the naked young boy lying facedown on the operating table and gagged. The skinny kid of no more than twelve was a mass of shredded skin and bloody ground beef from his buttocks to the nape of his neck. His head was swathed in bandages already. Helen moved around to the other side to start irrigating the cruel lacerations again as she told him quietly, "Barbwire. The father lashed him to a corral post and whipped him with a loop of barbwire. He's suffering concussion, too, thank God. He may not have felt all of it. Apparently the fun began with a good punch from the brute's fist. The mother managed to stop him just in time, I hope. I'm not sure he's going to make it, Matt. He's lost an awful lot of blood, and you can see he was malnourished to begin with."

Taylor growled deep in his throat and said, "It's my fault. I might have stopped it. But I never."

She said, "Inga told me. What are you going to do about it *now*?"

He said, "What *needs* to be done, of course," and turned on his heel to rejoin the women out front. He removed his hat to gently question the boy's mother.

Inga shook her head and said, "She's in shock. Helen gave her something. But it doesn't seem to be helping much. As far as we can put it together, two smaller children are still *out* there with that monster!"

He nodded and said, "I'm on my way," and ran out the door. His pony was at the livery at the far end of town. He untethered the buckboard team and climbed up on the seat, whipping them to action with the reins as he called out, "Let's go home, mules!"

Fortunately, he knew the general direction, and there could only be so many homesteads over that way. He swung around the first turn, drove the team across the cattle trail onto open prairie, and, spying a dot of light in the distance, made for it. It took forever before the dot of light became the open doorway of a sod house with a lamp lit inside. As he drove into the dooryard he heard a little kid crying. He reined in, rolled off the seat, and made for the house, gun drawn, as he called out, "Hatfield, this is the law. I'm coming in armed, so behave yourself, hear?"

But when he got inside the little one-room soddy he saw the crying was coming from a toddler in a corner crib. It looked more scared than hurt. A little girl of about five was seated on the floor in one corner, staring up at him owl-eyed. He smiled at her uncertainly and said, "Howdy, sis. Are you all right?"

The little girl nodded shyly and said, "Poppa was spanking Mammy. Tommy tried to make him stop and they all went outside. When are they coming back, mister? Baby sister is scared."

He said, "Well, I can see you're a big brave girl. You just find her bottle or something and I'll be right back, hear?"

She said they didn't have any food left and that that was why Pappy had been spanking Mammy. He told her to go give the baby a big hug at least, and moved back outside, cautiously.

He called out more than once. To no avail. Then he recalled what he'd been told about corral posts. He eased around the soddy to where he could make out corral poles in the dim light. Then he spotted someone lying prone in the dust near the corral, and moved in, saying, "On your feet, you no-good son-of-a-bitching baby beater!"

He got no answer. It was easy to see why, once he hunkered down for a better look. The blade of the ax was

imbedded deep in the back of the dead man's skull. He
whistled and told the cadaver, "You got off too easy, you
infernal animal."

He didn't need that sissy English gent, Sherlock Holmes,
to help him put the simple picture together. He needed
serious legal advice if there was to be any justice in this
world. He went back inside to find the little girl trying to
comfort the bawling toddler without much luck. He rummaged through the cupboard above the cold stove. The little
girl had been right about bare cupboards. Almost bare,
leastways. He found half a box of brown sugar, some
breadcrumbs, and, to no surprise at all, a jar of white
lightning, a quarter full. He poured the brown sugar into the
corn liquor, topped it with pump water he found by a corner
sink, and stirred it into a sickly-sweet goo he figured ought
to read about fifty proof, with the water added. He called
the little girl over, handed her the jar along with the
tablespoon he'd used to stir it with, and told her, "This may
taste funny. But it's good for you. Why don't you feed some
to your kid sister and drink some yourself whilst Uncle Matt
tends just a few more chores, hear?"

She sniffed at the contents, opined it smelled like Pappy's
medicine, and rejoined her little sister by the crib, saying,
"Look what I got for us!"

Taylor scooped up some bedding, carried it out to the
buckboard, and tossed it on the wagon bed. Then he led the
team afoot as close as he could manage to the corral. One of
the mules spooked at the scent of blood. He calmed it and
made sure they were both tethered good before he moved
over the body, picked it up, ax and all, and got it aboard,
wrapped in a dirty sheet. Then he went back inside, picked
up a shovel in one hand and the smallest child with the
other, and told the other child to follow him with the jar.
She did so, walking sort of funny as she asked him,
trustingly, where they were going. He told her they were
going to find her mommy. That helped a lot. But he still

wondered, as he nested the two bitty kids in blankets under the spring seat, whether he'd overdone that sweet drink he'd whipped up for them. As they started out, the wee one was already out like a light. The older one asked, sleepily, where Pappy was. He didn't tell her. She soon dozed off, lulled by the warmth of the bedding and the swaying of the buckboard as well as the hooch he'd fed her.

So as soon as they got to the cattle trail, he reined in, moved around to the back, and started digging. The first foot or so was easy, thanks to the way many a cow had churned up the soil with its hooves. After that the digging got tougher. But he knew he had to get down at least a yard, so he did. Then he dropped the dead man in the hole and covered him back up. The soil was a mite mounded where the late wife beater lay, but a few rains and even one herd of cows would put that to rights. He found the children still asleep as he climbed back up and drove on into town with them.

The beaten nester woman was no help at all in putting the two little girls to bed in one of the back rooms of the clinic. It was Helen, of course, who asked, "Did you find them in this state, Matt? If they weren't so tiny, I would swear they were *drunk*!"

He shrugged. and said, "Don't worry about 'em. They are. I found 'em hungry and hystericated, so I figured a little shot might cheer 'em up."

They both called him a fool, but Inga, at least, seemed to think it a mite funny. Helen said, "Well, I'm going to have enough on my hands when both that boy and his poor mother get over the shots I gave *them*. Where's the body, Matt? In the buckboard out front?"

He looked innocent and replied, "What body? All I found out to the Hatfield place was these two scared kids. I figure the old devil must have run off after giving his boy such a licking. I know *I* sure would."

The two girls exchanged odd looks. Then Inga said, "Matt, the woman says she hit her husband with an ax to keep him from killing her son."

He shrugged and said, "Well, you both told me she was in a state of shock, and who can blame her? If she hit him at all, I don't see how she could have hit him hard enough to even hurt him bad. Like I said, he'd run off by the time I could get out there."

This time he had to meet their gazes as they both stared up at him the same way. It was surprising that two young gals who didn't look at all alike could stare at a man the same thoughtsome way. Helen broke the silence by saying, "I see. She must have just imagined she hurt him with that ax." And Inga, bless her, agreed, "Everyone knows how hard it is to hurt a drunk. Ah, can we assure the poor woman he's not likely to come back and bother her again, Matt?"

He nodded soberly and said, "From the looks of things, he just ran off far and wide. I somehow doubt she'll ever see him anymore. The boy ought to be old enough to help run the place, if he lives."

Helen said, "I think he's going to. Those barbwire cuts were nasty, but not as deep as I feared. So we seem to be out of the woods now, right?"

Inga said, "It's our words against her confused memories, if push comes to shove. Is there anything I can do to help here, Helen?"

The lady M.D. shook her head and said, "No. With the whole family drunk or sedated, thanks to this odd cowboy nanny here, there's nothing for anyone to do but wait them out. It was kind of you to offer, though. I suppose Matt ought to see you safely home at this hour."

She sounded like she meant it. Taylor didn't want her madder at him than she already seemed to be. So he took Inga's arm and they left the clinic together. Inga waited until they'd walked a ways before she sighed and said, "Poor thing. She's really got it bad for you, you know."

He gulped and protested, "That's just *loco*, Miss Inga. She's *sore* at me for some fool reason. Don't ask me why. I've never *done* nothing to her."

Inga sighed again and said, "I know. You strong, silent types drive us women batty."

He smiled sheepishly and said, "I must be doing *something* wrong, judging from the odd things women keep saying to me. I didn't know you two gals knew one another, Miss Inga."

She replied, "Two spinster gals in a town this size? Surely you jest. Of course Helen and I are chums. Did you think I was just guessing when I said she was stuck on you?"

He said, "Well, I never. A gent I know was talking about that not long ago. He said gals who admire a gent are often prone to treat him mean. He said it's when a gal don't really care that she's *nice* to you. So I reckon that means you and me are just going to be pals, huh?"

She laughed and said, "Don't bet on that, cowboy. Helen saw you first. But there are limits to any small-town girl's loyalties when she finds herself my age, still single, and her girlfriend keeps acting like a little fool!"

The days wore on and then some. Nobody worried about another big herd coming up the Ogallala Trail that fall for the very same reason they were concerned about Big Bill Burton getting back. The climate of the High Plains west of, say, longitude 100 degrees paid less attention to the calendar than it did the uncertain winds blowing from any and all directions with nothing to slow wind down for many a mile. It was an election year, but the folk who'd settled on November for such get-togethers had done so back east, where the year had four predictable seasons. It was safe to bet on dry heat in August and dry cold in January on the High Plains. But after that all bets were off. For instead of fall or spring, the open prairie enjoyed a rapid-fire of hot and cold spells until it stayed hot or cold enough to call the result winter or summer. Folk neither voted nor traveled much once the fall winds commenced to shift about sort of sneaky. For a rider alone could get hit by a heat wave and a blizzard in the same day's ride, and that was providing he was lucky. In the so-called spring a hot chinook wind could fill all the draws with brawling snowmelt and force you to peel off your coat in the morning, only to pound you with hail and lightning bolts an hour later, if a twister roaring up from the south didn't carry you away, pony and all. A traveler alone on the prairie didn't have to worry as much about twisters in the so-called fall. At that time of the year the real killer was the wolf wind, as Indians called it, or the blue norther, as it was known to most stockmen. For while man or beast could usually survive an early blizzard, sheltered in a draw, the blue norther howled under a clear blue sky with no insulating snow to mention, cold enough to freeze whiskey in the jar. Tales were told of cattle, even horses and riders, found frozen stiff, still standing up, and many a nester family had frozen to death, inside, with a fire going in the stove, because their walls had been a mite thin and their fire a mite small. Nobody with a lick of sense traveled far from shelter until the winds had made up their minds whether it was summer or winter, and the county seat was almost a day's ride to the northwest. So Matt Taylor was getting so worried about old Big Bill getting back that he was tempted to ride over himself to see what could be keeping him. But that would have been dumb. So he didn't do it. He sent a Western Union message instead.

Big Bill didn't reply until the next day, saying the trial of Ben Fuller had been postponed again and that he wasn't about to see the Deleted-by-Western-Union go free as a bird, as he would, and as his slick lawyer *knew* he would, if there was nobody there to bear witness against him when he finally came to trial.

The mayor and city council didn't like it much. Mayor Smiley called Taylor in to fuss at him and his boss, saying, "Damn it, we don't pay Burton his handsome wages to enjoy the fall season amid the wicked delights of the county seat. He's supposed to be *here* when we need him!"

Taylor said soothingly, "We haven't even had to haul in half a dozen serious drunks since he's been gone, sir. With the drives over for the year, and the next payday a month away, you hardly need the services of us deputies."

Smiley grumbled, "We got Halloween coming, and you'd be surprised how big some kids can grow in these parts afore they lose interest in roping outhouses and shooting out window glass. We got the November elections to worry about as well. Barring a blue norther, folk for miles around will be crowding in to vote at the schoolhouse, and there's always trouble when you mix Democrats, Republicans, and Grangers with hard liquor in the same town."

Taylor nodded but said, "I'm sure Big Bill will be back by then, if only to vote for himself."

Smiley shook his head and said, "The position of town marshal ain't elective. We appoints him, and Burton's likely to get himself disappointed as hell if he don't get back here long before me and the boys are reelected."

Smiley shot Taylor a keen look from one little piggy eye as he added in a speculative tone, "You know, of course, that as only a deputy, you draw less'n half what you would as the marshal of our fair city?"

Taylor replied truthfully, "I hadn't thought about that much. What Big Bill might or might not make is his own beeswax to me."

The porky mayor said, "It ain't to us. We have to pay him, and it was you, not him, as foiled that robbery at my bank, as I have yet to forget, if you follow my drift."

Taylor did. He didn't like the way the conversation had

begun to drift. So he said, "It was Big Bill, not me, as shot it out with Fuller and Robles. Then he faced down the whole tough Circle Bar as well, remember?"

Smiley shrugged and said, "We was just talking about that at a council meeting the other day. Nobody can say Burton ain't brave. On the other hand, he'd have never had to *have* that fight if he hadn't made enemies of two boisterous cowhands in the first place. Any big man with a long-barreled gun can pistol-whip noisy cowhands. Your action in front of the bank that day was a damned fine job of law and order. It was mentioned at the meeting that more than one saloonkeeper admires your style at policing Main Street, too. They say you never come in waving your gun and enjoying a drink on the house as you warn one and all to behave themselves. They say you seldom come in at all. They say you can calm a noisy argument down by just standing in the doorway with that curious cold smile that makes drunks wonder if they may not just be a mite out of line. In sum, a lot of folk here in Freewater consider you the breed of professional peace officer a town like this *needs*."

Taylor smiled thinly and said, "I've been reading up on the law and I was brung up to know wrong from right. But if I've found it easy to keep the peace under Big Bill, it's only because Big Bill tamed this town in the first place. You might say some of his rep has run off on his deputies. Lord knows he's made it known far and wide that Freewater ain't a town to visit if the shooting out of street lamps is your main pleasure."

Smiley shook his fat pink head and said, "There's no reason for you to act so modest. You forget I own the bank, and that was a tidy sum you deposited with us when you got the bounty on those Redford brothers, you know. Anyone can see you're a lot younger as well as quieter than Burton, Matt. But don't think you haven't a rep of your own. It's quality rather than quantity that makes a lawman famous.

Nobody rightly recalls how many outlaws in all that the
famous Pat Garrett shot when he was sheriff of Lincoln
County, New Mexico, a dozen-odd years back. But they've
never forgotten he was the one as brought Billy the Kid to
justice. So far, old Bill Burton has yet to gun anyone as
important as the Redfords, and now he's wasting time over
to the county seat, trying to make a mean young cowboy
look more important than he ever was or ever could be.
How many infernal banks has the whole Circle Bar,
together, ever even tried to hold up?''

Taylor tried, "Ben Fuller's a born killer, sir. I was there
when he and Robles came up the street bold as brass, intent
on murder. After that I got to listen to him many a night in
his patent cell. He was just plain unrepentant and bragged
on more than one man he's killed down in Texas. I can
surely see why Big Bill wants the mean little cuss locked up
a spell.''

Smiley snorted in disgust and insisted, "He's still just
scum. There's at least one such bully in every outfit that
passes this way. Anyone can say he's killed a man, or a
polar bear for that matter. Most young cowboys would
rather admit to being virgins than being a sissy who's never
killed anybody, and I know for a fact that they don't get laid
as often as they like to let on.''

Taylor chuckled and said, "I know. I've been herding
cows since afore I knew why boys and gals was built
different. But I still say Fuller's the real thing.'' Then, since
he could see his defense of Big Bill wasn't going too well
with the fat little big shot, he tried, "Speaking of cowboys
getting laid, I thought the city council had agreed to wait till
Big Bill got back afore they brung up that notion of taxing
the east end again.''

Mayor Smiley laughed sheepishly and said, "You won
that chip in the end, son. I'll allow that after you'd sassed us
and left, we took a vote on whether to fire you or not. Some

of the boys was sore as hell at you. But most took the position that you could be right and that a lawman with the backbone to enforce the law as he saw it, and to hell with the consequences, was worth more to the town than mayhaps getting a few bucks off them whores, only to have some outlaws rob us blind, with a wishy-wash looking the other way. You're a born lawman, Matt. You got guts and you got honesty. We could start you at, say, two-thirds what we've been paying Burton, if you want his job."

Taylor shook his head and said, "That wouldn't be honesty on anyone's part. Big Bill was the one as hired me to begin with. He never hired me to steal his job, and even if he had, I'd be a fool to work for less. Is that what you and the council are truly after, a chance to get a cut-rate marshal who'd stab a pal in the back?"

Mayor Smiley sighed and said, "Maybe Dick the barber is right. You're just too damned ethical for anyone's good. But that damned Bill Burton better get back here sudden, just the same."

Taylor knew he meant it. So he left to go directly to the Western Union office to send another wire on the subject. The dinky small-town telegraph office was run by an old gent who'd been owl-eyed before he ever bought those horn-rimmed specs. He said he'd be proud to send another wire to Marshal Burton over at the county seat, but added that he found this a mite confusing, since the U.S. Marshal's office in Denver had just sent Big Bill a wire in care of Freewater. Taylor said he was acting as marshal while Big Bill was away. So after making him sign for it, the old-timer handed over the sealed yellow envelope.

Taylor tore the wire open to read:

INFORMANT REPORTS REDFORD GANG HOLED UP IN OR ABOUT FREEWATER STOP ADVISE EXTREME CAUTION STOP MAY BE AFTER DEPUTY TAYLOR STOP MARSHAL LONG DENVER DISTRICT COURT.

Taylor whistled softly and said, "Don't send what I just wrote. I got to reword it." Then he did, informing Big Bill he'd wait until his boss got back before he made a sweep of the unseemly parts of town. The clerk read it, gasped, and said, "Yep, that'll have him back here within the day, Buntline Special cocked, if I know Big Bill Burton!"

Taylor left to scout up the other deputies. He found Joe Walsh in the Bull-Head and told him to track down Tim Hogan and meet him at the lockup. Then he went to the lockup, unlocked it, and sat down to wait, cleaning one of the ten-gauges as he sat there.

Joe Walsh came in almost an hour later, looking upset. He said, "It's gétting sort of nipsome out there. You reckon we're in for an early frost, Matt?"

Taylor said, "I don't think so. The wind's too far to the west. Where's Tim?"

Joe Walsh moved over to the gun rack, hauled out a shotgun for himself, and took a seat by the window, saying, "He ain't coming. I told him you and Big Bill would be mighty vexed with him if he chose a time like this to turn in his badge. But he's got this young gal he's fixing to marry up with, and, well, he said your feud with the Redford brothers wasn't his fight."

Taylor went on cleaning the ten-gauge as he said, "I see. What about you, Joe? Do you want out?"

Walsh sighed and said, "I sure do. I don't like the notion of you and me against the Redford boys at all. But you'd be in even a worse fix if *I* crawfished out on you, too. So, dumb as it may be, here I am. What do we do now, Matt?"

Taylor said, "We wait for Big Bill. By now he'll have got my wire, and it's brisk enough outside for hard riding. He ought to make it before sundown. If the Redfords are really in town, and willing to attack in broad daylight, they'd have likely done so by now. They'd have had me cold, up until a few minutes ago. So I figure they're either not here at all or waiting for dark."

Joe Walsh loaded the shotgun, but felt too butterflied to clean it, apparently. His voice was steady, though, in the way a good soldier's voice stays steady when he's really worried, as he opined, "If I was you, I'd consider deputizing some extra help about now, Matt."

Taylor shook his head and explained, "Good help can be hard to find at short notice. I don't know the others here in town well enough to say who'd get overanxious and trigger-happy or mayhaps take Tim's attitude a mite less honestly. I'd rather not count on a man at all than count on him only to have him run out on me at the last moment. That's what they say happened at the O.K. Corral that time, you know. Six old boys rode into town to dare Marshal Virgil Earp to a fight. Then, at the last minute, three of 'em just ran away, leaving the other three to fight and lose."

Walsh nodded and said, "Big Bill told me that story, too. If he gets back in time, it'll be the three of us against the two of them, though, right?"

Taylor replied soberly, "I don't know. The federal marshal in Denver never said if it was just the two brothers left or if they brung some backup. The gang can't be too big, though. They'll have learned they only have three lawmen to deal with. If there was much more than that on the other side, we'd have heard from them by now. Nobody has ever accused the Redford boys of having chicken livers or even common sense. I wish that damned Hogan had at least come by, though. I could have sent him over to alert the bank guards, whether he wanted to fight or not."

Walsh peered out the window and said, "This cold has most of the town indoors. But I see a kid coming down the street. Want me to hail him in so's you can use him as a messenger boy?"

Taylor said, "No. I don't want anyone who ain't paid by the township taking risks for the same. I saw a kid get hurt just a few nights ago, and it made me feel sick as hell."

Walsh said, "We heard the boy's going to be all right, though. Has anyone said yet where that ornery Hatfield might have run off to?"

Taylor inserted two monstrous shells into the now clean shotgun, snapped it shut, and placed it on the desk in front of him as he replied casually, "Nobody that knows where he might be has seen fit to report it. The family will be staying in town a spell. So why worry about it?"

Walsh said, "Oh-oh, someone's coming, Matt." So Taylor rose, scooped up the scattergun, and joined Walsh at the window. Then he saw it was the fancy dan called Marcel, who worked for Freewater Fannie, and opened the door to let the pimp in.

Marcel shot a knowing look at the shotguns both lawmen were holding, muzzles politely down, and said, "I can see you heard. Miss Fannie wants to know how much backup you want. We can loan you half a dozen gun hands, Matt."

Taylor smiled thinly and replied, "That's mighty neighborly of you all, Marcel. I hope you won't feel insulted if I decline such a kind offer. It just don't seem right to deputize one mess of crooks to fight another mess of crooks, though."

Marcel smiled boyishly and said, "She said you'd say that. I had to hear it for myself. Me and the boys are neither as downright nasty as Jeb and Winslow Redford nor dumb enough to twist your arm. Just remember the offer was made, if you live out the night, and good luck, you windmill-fighting cuss."

Taylor thanked Marcel for his kindly thought and added, "I don't suppose you'd like to tell us how many of them there are and where they might be right now?"

To which Marcel replied, "I'd like to. I can't. If they was enjoying the delights of our own establishment, we'd have no problem at all to discuss. It's surprising what a gal on good terms with the town law can do to a man she has in her wicked power. They're holed up in another house my code forbids me to name for the law. I can say the madam ain't on such good terms with Big Bill and you boys as Miss Fannie is. She's taken the position that it's dumb to take sides. But we're sort of nosy. So as far as we know, you just have the two brothers to deal with. If they keep drinking, they may not be much of a problem for anyone. If they come at you half-sober, you really ought to reconsider Miss Fannie's offer. Jeb Redford is bad enough. Winslow likes to show off by driving nails into tree trunks from across the street."

Taylor said he'd remember that. Marcel said, "You'd better. By the way, Jeb Redford's southpaw. So he sidewinds right when he draws. He's the skinny one. Winslow just stands there. I'd aim for him first if I was you."

They shook on it friendly, and the fancy dan left. Joe Walsh said flatly, "Matt, that was dumb as hell. That old boy and his pals are real good gun-slicks."

Taylor said, "I know. They're pimps and worse as well. How would it look if Freewater hired such disgusting help?"

Walsh insisted, "Virgil Earp wasn't too proud to ask old Doc Holliday for help, down Tombstone way that time."

But Taylor just shrugged and said, "My name ain't Virgil Earp. At least one of his kid brothers was a pimp as well. So mayhaps he didn't see the difference. You got to do things lawful if you mean to fight in the name of the law, Joe. You can still leave, if I'm too honest for you."

Walsh laughed bitterly and said, "I consider you more foolish than honest. But what the hell; if I got to die, never let it be said I wasn't killed in a fair fight. What time do you figure Big Bill might get here, Matt?"

Taylor shot a glance at the wall clock before he said, "Six or seven hours, if he ain't too easy on his pony. Longer if he lets it walk all that much."

Walsh glanced outside again to observe, "The sky's still

clear, and the few clouds up yonder ain't moving. It's just right for hard riding. But what if he don't come at all?"

"It'll still be two against two, won't it?" Taylor muttered.

Walsh said, "Not hardly. I know this is a hell of a time to mention it, Matt. But I've never been in a real gunfight before."

Taylor said, "Settle down and try to relax, Joe. There has to be a first time for all of us. But you won't be much help to me if you fall apart before it comes time to see to your education."

Days were supposed to get shorter in the fall. But that one seemed to last forever before the sun began to go down. By that time everyone in town knew the Redford boys were supposed to be in town. So business along Main Street was so slow that many a shop closed early. Big Bill hadn't shown up by sundown. Helen Harris did, carrying her black bag as she marched up to the front door and demanded to be let in. Taylor opened the door. She was even less safe out there with her fool back to the whole town. He said, "This is no place for ladies right now, even if you are a lady doctor."

She said, "Pooh, I have to get into a bullet wound right away if I'm to do any good at all." Then she looked around the unlit office to add thoughtfully, "I only see two of you here, Matt. Where are the others?"

He said, "They couldn't make it. What say you leave us some bandages and that bottle of snakebite medicine and just go on home, Miss Helen? Joe and me ain't planning all that anxious on getting shot; and if *you* got shot, neither of us would know what to do about it, see?"

She snapped, "I see all too well that your big brave Bill Burton has let you down. *He* must have heard the Redford boys were in town, too. I'll just put my bag here on his desk, and now I'll thank you to issue me a gun. Might you have a twelve-gauge, Matt? I find those big market-hunter's cannon a mite hard to handle with the wrists God gave me."

He laughed incredulously and said. "We don't keep any schoolgirl guns on hand here, Miss Helen. If we did, you still couldn't have one. I want you to run along, now, while there's still time. I mean that, Helen."

She moved over to the gun rack, got herself a ten-gauge, and broke it open to load in a manner that hinted at more experience in such matters than your average Gibson Girl. She snapped it shut and said, "All right. Where's my station and why are the windows still shut? Don't you know anything about flying glass?"

They both laughed. Then Joe Walsh explained, "It's nippy out, ma'am. There's no sense catching a chill afore we know for sure them Redford boys is in town, see?"

Taylor said, "Goddamn it, Helen, stay clear of them windows, at least. I'll tell you what. Why don't you sort of hunker down ahint the desk if you're just too stubborn to leave us men be?"

She nodded, carried her shotgun over, and sat down in Big Bill's chair, saying, "All right. I can get anyone coming through the door just as well from here. I hope it's that glandular case who got you poor boys into this fix in the first place!"

Taylor, positioned near the right window as it got ever darker outside, said, "Them's hard words, Doc. The Redfords are after *me*, personal, and it ain't Big Bill's fault they chose to come at a time they must have known he'd be out of town."

She asked, "Don't you mean he'd just as likely heard they might be coming?" To which he had to reply, "That's just plain unjust. We just today got the tip by wire. The Marshal's been gone for days. He'll get back in time, if he can. So go easy with that scattergun when he does. I don't see why you're so sore at him to begin with, Doc. What's he ever done to you?"

She said, "Nothing. I've had the joy of treating some of the cowboys he's pistol-whipped or worse. The man's a natural bully and, as you can see, a four-flusher as well."

He started to point out that he'd been there the time Big Bill had proven that last accusation wrong. But someone was coming, a shabby drunk he'd seen around town many a time. They called him Corks, and he was known to be harmless. So Taylor opened the door to say, "Evening, Corks. If you need a warm cell to bed down in, the answer has to be no right now."

The old drunk replied, "That ain't why I come. I was sent. Two young gents was just asking for you at the Palm Court Saloon. The one called Winslow said you'd know what they wanted if I'd be kind enough to tell you they was there."

Taylor thought. He knew the Palm Court was across from the Bull-Head, near the Ogallala Trail, where the street-lights sort of thinned out. He hauled Corks inside and demanded, "Spell it out a mite more, Corks. Just the two of 'em, forted up in the saloon?"

The old-timer nodded but said, "Don't go, son. They've been drinking and they look mean as anything."

Taylor decided, "They must be drunk indeed. Which side of the front door would they be on as one was going in, Corks?"

The drunk said, "To your right, away from the bar, at a corner table near the piano. The piano player left when they come in. I had to come and tell you. They told me to. But now that I'm out of there, I feels honor-bound to tell you not to go meet 'em. I don't think they could be friends of your'n, Deputy Taylor."

Taylor said, "I know who they are. You go back and flop in the cell that ain't locked, Corks." Then he turned to his only backup and said, "Joe, I want you to fort up here with Miss Helen and tell Big Bill where I've gone when he gets here."

Helen and Walsh gasped as one and both shouted, "No!" at the same time. Walsh added, "Wait for the boss. He could be here any minute!"

But Taylor explained, "The Redford brothers could be somewhere else by then. I know what I'm doing. There's a back door to the Palm Court, and if they're forted in a corner staring at the front door, they must be drunk to the point of harmless. I'd best round 'em up now, lest I never get as fine a chance."

All three of them kept bitching at him as Taylor left, shotgun carried across his chest at port arms. He moved directly across the street to duck into the first slot between the frame walls. He knew that even if the Redfords hadn't actually posted any lookouts, some born troublemaker was ever anxious to run down the street ahead, shouting, "Here he comes!"

He made it back to the alley running all the way to the cattle trail behind the buildings fronting Main Street. It was paved with a little gravel and a lot of horse shit, all frozen pretty solid, bless the oncoming winter. He didn't crunch any more than he had to as he strode down the dark alley. Since he wasn't all that anxious to get where he had to go, it seemed no time at all before he was behind the Palm Court Saloon. A cat or a mighty big rat darted away from the garbage cans out back as Taylor paused to decide his next move. The back door was open. He could see a dimly lit and narrow passage led forward to the main spread up front. If the Redfords were still where Corks had said he'd last seen them, they'd be directly to his left as he busted through to them. He took a deep breath and made ready to charge on in. But then all hell busted loose at once.

Taylor leaped halfway out of his socks as two pistol shots

went off directly behind him. He came down facing the other way just in time to blow Jeb Redford almost in two at the waist no matter who it might be. Then he spun down to one knee, aiming the other way, as Winslow Redford ran out the back door and managed to yell, "Did you get him?" before Taylor emptied the other barrel of the ten-gauge into his face, tearing his head off in the process. Then, before the headless body could hit the floor inside, Taylor was hunkered in the darkest corner he could find, his .44–40 in hand, as he heard the soft crunch of leather on gravel. It wasn't the first one he'd shot. There was just enough light to see that one sprawled in a spreading puddle of blood and torn-up bowels. A familiar voice called out, "Hold your fire, Taylor. It's me, Marcel DuVal."

The bewildered young deputy stayed put, calling back, "Show yourself, hands friendly, then."

So the fancy dan stepped into view above the torn-up corpse, his gun back under his frock coat, as he said, "This one's Jeb. The one inside would be old Winslow. Nice shooting, pard."

Taylor rose, but kept the six-gun in his right hand leveled as he held the empty ten-gauge in his left. He said, "That sure was dumb of me. They no doubt figured no lawman with a lick of sense would respond to their invite by coming in the front way."

Marcel said indifferently, "We live and learn. Since they was after you, it was easy enough for me to keep an eye on 'em as they left the red-light district. I'd have gunned Jeb for you sooner if you hadn't acted so stubborn. I didn't think you'd mind if I nailed him just as he was throwing down on your fool back."

Taylor gulped and said, "I thought that was *him* shooting just now. Since I'm still alive, I have to allow I didn't mind at all. But which one of us would you credit the bastard to, Marcel?"

The pimp chuckled and said, "He's all yours, lawman. I get tired of having to change my name every time I have one of these discussions. I hope you know that you're stuck with a real rep as a gunslinger now."

As they both heard the growing rumble of cautious but curious townsfolk moving in from all sides for a look-see at who might have won, Taylor holstered his .44–40 and held out his hand to say, "I owe you, Marcel." But the pimp replied, "It was on the house, courtesy of Miss Freewater Fannie, and so I'll be on my way before anyone asks me for my autograph. The whole damn Redford gang is all yours."

Taylor said, "Hold on. There's bounty money on both these old boys we got betwixt us, Marcel."

But the pimp shook his head and faded back into the darkness as he said, "I don't have your hunting license. I ain't anxious to get back-shot by some fool kid out to build his *own* rep, neither. My chosen field is dangerous enough, thank you very much."

Big Bill Burton didn't come back to Freewater for two more days. By which time the excitement had died down considerable. The giant marshal insisted on taking Taylor to the Prairie Dog to celebrate the victory anyway, calling out for drinks all around as he slapped Taylor on the back again and said, "You done us all proud, old son. They even run the story in the *Denver Post*. I knew you had the makings of a lawman in you, and at the rate you're going, you'll soon be famous as me!"

Taylor waited until everyone had been served and he'd shaken all the hands stuck out at him before he drew his boss to one side and said, "Pay attention for a change, Big Bill. If you heard about me and the Redford brothers all the way over to the county seat, you must have heard some of the mean-mouthing about yourself that went with it. I want you to know up front that I never started it. If you couldn't get back that night, you must have had your own good reasons. That's all I've said to anyone who's asked."

Big Bill inhaled some suds, slammed down his schooner, and said, "Hell, kid, I know who my friends are. I know who's been after the city council to get rid of me, too. They've been mean-mouthing me since long afore I hired you. I had my own good reasons for sticking tight as a tick to the county courthouse gang."

Taylor said cautiously, "We heard Ben Fuller was convicted and given ten at hard, the day before I sent you that wire, boss."

Big Bill said, "I know. I was there. The reason I was too busy to come back is that I had bigger fish to fry. Would you like my job here in Freewater, old son?"

Taylor said, "Damn it, I'm not after your job, and you know it! But *somebody* else is likely to wind up with it if you don't spend a mite more *time* at it."

Big Bill said, "I can't. I'm running for county sheriff as a last-minute write-in. I told you I'd been making friends over to the county seat. The old fart running for reelection ain't never done squat since he took office four long years ago."

Taylor whistled softly and said, "You surely *must* have had a few drinks in a smoke-filled room! But ain't it mighty late to get on the ticket? You're more famous here than in any other part of the county, and while the sheriff they've got hasn't had to deal with trail drives through the county seat, he ain't done nothing wrong, as far as I've heard tell."

Big Bill nodded and said, "That's what I just said. He ain't done *nothing*. So some say it's time they had a real sheriff."

He looked around as if to make sure he wasn't being overheard as he confided, "You're welcome to this job in Freewater. You may even get it, when Smiley and his pals are voted out. Everybody seems to like you. But I know that if the pettifogging *reformers* take over Freewater, *my* days here will be numbered short as hell."

Taylor smiled incredulously and said, "You're talking foolish. Smiley's party is sure to win again. It's barely a month to election time, and so far, I haven't even seen a political poster up yet."

Big Bill shrugged and said, "Being dumb goes with getting smug. There's never a big turnout, with most of the country folk worried about getting snowed in any minute. Smiley never bothers to campaign. He figures being the banker is all it takes. Meanwhile, the other side's started a whispersome campaign. The mean things you've heard about me are only part of it. I've yet to be accused of half the things old Smiley has. Either way, the office of county sheriff is a step up as well as more certain. So just go on being nice to everyone, and once I'm elected to higher office, they'll likely appoint you the town marshal no matter who wins, hear?"

Taylor grimaced and said, "I wish I had your ears, Big Bill. Nobody's told me any of this stuff. So how do you stay so well informed when you ain't even here?"

Big Bill chuckled and said, "Freewater Fannie just told me how prim you act around whores. I just came from her parlor house because it's nice to warm up after a long, cold ride. Half the men in town get laid at Freewater Fannie's, regular. So you'd be surprised how much her sweet sassy-gals hear about the inner workings of this town."

Taylor said, "No I wouldn't. I'm probably still breathing right now because that redhead felt obliged to save me from my own foolishness the other night. But whorehouse gossip is one thing, and the ballot box is another. Men talk foolish as well as a lot when they're drinking with soiled doves. I wouldn't bet my job on such talk if I was you."

Big Bill replied expansively, "I ain't. I see the connections I've made at county level as a no-lose game, old son.

Why should I try to please a mess of reformsome sissies or even the rascals helping Smiley run this one-hoss town when I don't have to? I don't care who wins here, as long as my party wins the county, come November."

Taylor said he didn't care if Big Bill didn't care. Then he said, "Afore you go running off to kiss babies again, I'd like to know what you think we ought to do about Tim Hogan. I told you in the report I mailed you how he'd let us down when the Redford brothers come to town, remember?"

Big Bill shrugged and said, "I told you when I hired you that the boys I had wasn't worth spit. I'm surprised Joe Walsh showed as much grit as he did. There ain't much we can do about Tim. I was told to hire him as a favor to an uncle he has on the city council. Trying to fire him would just raise more of a fuss than the cowardly cuss is worth, Matt."

Taylor sipped some beer before he said, "You're the boss. With Halloween coming, we can likely have Tim guard the windows along Main Street from kids with soap. That's assuming he ever reports for duty again, of course. I haven't seen him since he crawfished on Joe and me."

Big Bill said, "I'll have a word with him. I can't be here for Halloween myself. Got to ride about the other townships and belly up to the bar with old boys who don't know me as well as you."

Taylor frowned and said, "I just allowed you were the boss. But, no bull, do you think that's fair to me and Joe?"

Big Bill grinned sheepishly and said, "No, but rank has its privileges, old son. Look at it another way. You're sure to get the job I hold now if the whole town sees you doing all the work, right?"

Taylor could only look disgusted as he finished his drink and signaled the barkeep for a round on him. But before they could be served, the frock-coated Marcel DuVal came

in, spotted them, and moved over to join them, saying,
"Bill, we got a dead body on our hands. Thought you ought
to know."

Big Bill laughed and said, "It was neighborly of you to
tell me, Frenchy. Who killed him or her, and where?"

Marcel said, "Nobody killed him. He just died. Miss
Fannie said you'd understand it would look better if you
wrote it down, official, that he died out front in the street."

Big Bill said that sounded reasonable. But Taylor said,
"Hold on. It's up to Doc Crane, the deputy coroner here in
Freewater, to record such matters for the county, ain't it?"

Big Bill explained, "He's been reading books, Frenchy."

But the pimp looked more annoyed than enlightened as
he said, "We sent for the old quack. Miss Fannie said we
ought to tell the law as well. Had it been up to me alone,
we'd have just buried the cuss out on the prairie. But you
know how delicate she is."

Big Bill sighed and said, "Well, we'd best have a look at
the remains, at least. Where's he at, the cathouse?"

Marcel shook his head and said, "Not hardly. We sent
him over to the wagon wright's so's he can be certified
and measured for a box at the same time. Miss Fannie says
she'll pay for it. Him being such a regular customer and
all."

The three of them left for the closer business establishment. As they walked the short way, Big Bill casually asked
who the late lamented might have been. Marcel replied,
"They called him Fats. Last names ain't asked in the east
end of town. The nickname fit him, as you'll see. I think he
worked as a cowhand for some spread a piece out of town.
Him and his pals only got in once a week."

Taylor asked how many pals they were talking about and
if and why they'd run off to leave a sidekick dead or dying.
Big Bill asked what difference that made. But Marcel said,
"The same thought occurred to Miss Fannie. They might

not have wanted it known where they spent their time in town. One of the gals who knew them better, in the biblical sense, said she thought she'd heard one of 'em brag on the eight-oh-something brand."

Big Bill got a chance to prove he was smart by saying flatly, "There's no such brand in these parts. Your gal got it wrong or else they was greening her, Frenchy."

Marcel sighed and said, "I wish you'd quit calling me Frenchy and calling them whores my girls. In the first place, I'm Canadian, and in the second, I don't peddle pussy."

Big Bill laughed and insisted, "You guard such goods for old Fannie, don't you? What kind of a name is Marcel if it ain't as French as French Fifi's tricks at your cathouse?"

The fancy dan swore in Red River French and said, "One of these days, Burton. I may not always be working for your pal, Miss Fannie, you know."

Big Bill laughed again and said, "Oh Lord, you're scaring me half to death. Was you always so ferocious or did you pick it up from herding whores so many a year?"

Marcel didn't answer. Taylor felt embarrassed for both of them. Then they'd made it to the open front of the wagon wright's and went on back to the workshop, where the town's only undertaker and the old quack who doubled as deputy coroner when he wasn't treating the denizens of the red-light district for the clap or worse were jawing over a body lying on two planks across a team of sawhorses. The dead man was wearing unbuttoned jeans and an open hickory shirt. The feet were bare. It was easy to see why they'd called him Fats. He must have weighed close to three hundred pounds. His pudgy face was disfigured by a ghastly grin.

Big Bill said, "I thought you said he just died, Frenchy. That death grin don't set in for hours, as a rule."

Doc Crane said, "It's not rigor, Marshal. It seems he

liked to inspire himself with strychnine tonic before he went up to the cribs with one or more gals."

Big Bill asked, "Are you saying this was suicide, then, Doc?"

Crane shook his head and explained. "Strychnine only kills you if you overdo it. In moderation, mixed with water and a little sloe gin, it can give a man one hell of an erection. This fat boy must have needed such inspiration. He'd sure let himself go to pot. Trying to take on two gals at once would have been hard enough on the poor lard's ticker. Getting it up for two gals with the help of strychnine tonic was just plain stupid. But that's the way some gents are. I'm putting it down to heart failure, which is the simple truth, when you study on it. We wouldn't want to cause trouble for our neighborhood druggist, would we?"

Big Bill agreed that sounded reasonable and turned to Taylor to add, "We've seen the dead bastard. If the doc says he died natural, there's nothing else for us to do here, Matt."

But Taylor said, "Hold on. Ain't we supposed to try and find out who he was afore we plant him, boys?"

Big Bill shrugged and said, "His name was Fats. What more do you want? If his pals gave a hang about him, poor Miss Fannie wouldn't be stuck with paying the planting charges. I don't see why *we* should worry about him if the pals he rode to town with don't. He was likely just a sort of disgusting saddle tramp in life as well as death, see?"

Taylor shook his head and said, "I just read a library book on proper peace officer procedure, boss. No offense, but we ain't supposed to just drop him in a hole in the ground, unknown and unrecorded."

Big Bill smiled crookedly and said, "Well, you record him all you want, Matt. I've had a hard day and I mean to get some shut-eye. But you be sure and wake me if he tells you anything at all important, hear?"

Then he left, muttering to himself about eager young-sters. So Taylor turned to the wagon wright–cum–under-taker and asked if he had a pencil and paper handy. The shop owner rummaged about and found some brown wrapping paper and a carpenter's lead. Taylor took them with a nod of thanks and found a bare patch of workbench to write down "80?" and "Fats." Then he shot a harder look at the dead man's face and muttered, "We could be talking about that 808 trail herd that passed through earlier this fall. It's hard to tell, with his face all twisted up like that. But one of the Texas drovers I had trouble with, my first night in town, was a mighty fat rascal. Whatever happened to his hat, Marcel?"

The Canadian said, "French Fifi kept it as a memento of a long-lost love, most likely. I recall the 808 outfit coming through. They kept going. I don't see how this poor slob could have been left behind all this time."

Taylor said, "Try her this way. They drove the herd up to the Ogallala railyards and naturally got paid off. They all wore hats creased Texican. So they'd have headed south again, without the herd, right?"

Marcel said, "Sure. But that was weeks ago, Matt. All those old boys should have made it back to Texas by this time."

Taylor pointed his big pencil at the fat cadaver as he shook his head and said, "Not this one, and you say he was coming in once a week with others. How many others are we talking about?"

Marcel thought before he decided, "More than three and less'n half a dozen. Who counts hard-up cowhands?"

Taylor wrote down "4 or 5" and said, "This is starting to get interesting. Let's say some of the 808 riders found jobs in these parts as they was drifting home, disemployed. I've done the same in my time. But if they was working for some local spread, how come they said they still rode for the 808?"

Marcel shrugged and asked, "What does it matter? This one's dead, and his pals ought to turn up again, sooner or later. You can ask them when they come to town again."

Taylor frowned and pointed out, "*If* they come to town again, you mean. It ain't natural for honest hands to run off and leave a pard dead and untended. Ergo, they might not be all that honest."

Marcel said, "That works. What does ergo mean?" So Taylor was forced to smile sheepishly and say, "It's a fancy word I picked up from a book. Big Bill might have a point about my reading habits. To put it less fancy, men who don't want to talk to the law about a dead man they never killed might have something more important to hide."

The wagon wright nodded and said, "I follow your drift. In my time I've boxed and planted more than one old boy who died sort of mysterious. But this is the first time I've dealt with anyone who died natural without even a dog to mourn his passing."

Marcel said, "Well, it's a cold, cruel world out there, and an outlaw likes to get laid as much as most men. But if this one and his pals was crooks, shouldn't they have been crooking somebody? You'd know better than me if anyone was missing stock, or even laundry off their clothesline, wouldn't you?"

Taylor nodded and said, "It's been peaceable as anything in these parts since the last of the Redfords rode in. I can't see these mysterious strangers as part of the Redford gang. For had the gang been that big, Jeb and Winslow never would have come in alone that night."

Marcel asked, "Why couldn't they be *another* gang, hiding out around Freewater for whatever reason?"

And Taylor said, "You just stole the words right out of my mouth. Now all I have to do is figure out who and how come. Does this dead one have any other distinguishing features, save for his fat gut, Doc?"

Doc Crane said, "I can't say. Let's see," as he tore the dead man's duds looser.

Marcel sighed and said, "We'd have never gone to the trouble of getting him dressed again if we'd known you wanted him bare-ass. That was the condition he died in. French Fifi said she thought he was coming, but as it turned out, he was going. I hope you ain't writing that down, Matt."

Taylor chuckled and said, "Don't worry. I got to do this proper. But I see no good reason to be *prim* and proper."

Doc Crane said, "Well, he's been vaccinated twice. That could make him an old army man. Few cowhands bother with getting that done *once*. He's got an old bullet wound near his hipbone as well. It was lucky for him he was so fat. It doesn't look as if it was ever treated. I'd say the rifle round was still in him. Buffalo round, if you want an educated guess."

Taylor frowned and asked, "Can't you do better than *guess*, if you think the round's still *in* him, Doc?"

The old abortionist sighed and said, "You sure are nosy" before he reached down to the open medical kit on the dirt floor, got out a scalpel, and proceeded to slice the fat corpse open with an expression of bored indifference.

There wasn't much blood. But Taylor still had to swallow the green taste in his mouth as Crane went in with two fingers to grope about a spell before he brought them out, greasy, with a gory .50-caliber slug, saying, "I told you it was a buffalo round."

Taylor wrote that down. Then he said, "That ought to be enough for an all-points bulletin. Thanks, Doc."

Marcel asked what was all-points. So Taylor explained, "We send the description to all the main law offices that might be at all interested in a Texas rider found dead in

Colorado. If this cuss was wanted, serious, anywhere, they might be able to match up a mighty fat cuss with two vaccination scars and that old rifle wound."

"What if nobody can?" asked Marcel. To which Taylor could only reply, "Then we'll likely never know who this fat slob might have been. The point is, we're supposed to try."

All that happened for the next few days was that Big Bill rode off somewhere before Halloween, and thanks to a nicely timed cold snap, Halloween went unusually peaceful that year. They only had to haul in a couple of falling-down drunks and poor old Corks, lest they freeze to death.

Having spoiled the kids' fun, the weather turned mild again and everyone agreed that if the wind didn't shift again, they'd likely have a fine turnout for election day.

Inga Larsen mentioned this to Taylor one afternoon as he was trading in some books at the library. She said the election would be held over in the schoolhouse and that she'd feel safer if he or one of the other deputies stood by to see nobody ran off with the ballot box. He told her not to worry and asked, "Might you have any books by Professor Burlington, the Frenchman who's so good at measuring crooks?"

She dimpled up at him and said, "I think you must mean Bertillon, the criminologist, Matt. Where on earth did you hear about him and his methods?"

He said, "I read it in one of them detection books. Only, it failed to explain how the system worked. I'd sure like to read up on it from the horse's mouth."

She laughed and said, "I fear you've about outgrown our small-town library, Matt. We just don't have much call for scientific texts, and you've devoured those few we have. Who were you planning to measure according to the Bertillon system, anyway?"

He said, "Mysterious strangers, if and when I find any lurking about. It's just too easy for a crook to fib about his past. There has to be a way a lawman can compare notes with others when he has a suspect handy but can't prove who he might be for sure."

She nodded understandingly but said, "We're going to have to get you a mail-order list, then. I can't believe a man who was checking out children's books a few short weeks ago has advanced to such technical texts already!"

He shrugged and said, "I only admitted to dropping out of school sort of young. I never said I'd been kicked in the head by a mule."

"Your grammar is improving, too," she insisted, adding, "Nobody ever said you were stupid, Matt. I knew you were bright from the beginning. But to tell the truth, you're so bright it's a little frightening. It's no wonder so many folk have been saying you'd make a better town marshal than poor old Big Bill Burton."

He snorted in disbelief and said, "We could both be out of a job if them reform gents win the election."

She sighed and said, "I see you and Helen are talking again. I told her she was playing too hard to get."

He shot her a puzzled look and asked, "What has how me and the doc get along got to do with the fool election, Miss Inga?"

She asked, "Didn't you know Helen Harris is hoping and praying for a new mayor and town council, Matt?"

He replied, "I didn't even know ladies were allowed to vote in Colorado. Who are *you* fixing to vote for, Miss Inga?"

She made a wry face and said, "Alas, we girls are still waiting for such advances in these parts. But naturally the wives of this town have some influence on their menfolk. Those who have menfolk to influence, at any rate. As the only doctor in town a decent woman would go to, Helen is as mixed up in the reform movement as any woman can hope to be. But why am I telling you all this. Hasn't *she*?"

He shook his head and said, "Nope. Last time I spoke to her, I was trying to get her to put down a shotgun, without much luck. You still haven't told me who you'd vote for, if you could, Miss Inga."

She looked away to murmur, "You are persistent as well as sharp, aren't you? All right, if you must know, I owe my job and the new schoolhouse to Banker Smiley and his cronies. That might not stop me from voting against them, if I was allowed to vote and had good reason. But between you and me, I don't see how the fuddy-duddy old goats who preach against what they call the Smiley Gang could run things any better. Mayor Smiley has his faults, Lord knows, but he's never been caught with his hand in the till, he seems to be able to keep the riffraff out of this part of town, and you know what they say about the devil you know. The so-called reformers lost me when they said they'd close down all the saloons in town. It's not that I don't think they *should*. I just don't see how they *can*. So I don't think they really mean what they're saying."

He frowned thoughtfully and observed, "This town would go broke if they shut down the saloons and, like it or not, places even less seemly. Free water and expensive pleasures are all a trail town has going for it."

She nodded and insisted, "That's what I just said. Your Helen and I have had some swell arguments about that. She can afford to dwell in an ivory tower, treating the more respectable folk in Freewater. I can't seem to make her see that once you destroy the really profitable businesses in any town, the hat and notions merchants are the first to move away."

He nodded and said, "You don't sell much to country gals who come to town mayhaps four or five times a year. But where do you get off calling the doc *my* Helen? No offense, Miss Inga, but you're talking just dumb. I never said she was repulsive, I'll allow, but I'd sure look stupid courting high-toned ladies with college degrees. I'm just an old country boy and always will be."

She arched an eyebrow at him to reply, "False modesty ill becomes a man on the rise, Matt. You're as well educated as most of the leading merchants of this town, and at the rate you're going, you'll be the county sheriff before the turn of this century."

He laughed in disbelief and told her, "No I won't. Big Bill Burton figures to be the next sheriff. I'll be lucky if I wind up as high as town marshal."

She said, "Don't bet on it. Some say he's trying too hard. You might say courting the voters is a lot like courting a girl. It's not smart to appear too anxious. I have another book I'd like you to read. I think you're about ready for *The Prince*, by Niccolò Machiavelli. He was an Italian politician who took up writing after living through times much like our own, Matt. Politics out here can get just about as wild as they did in the days of the Renaissance bullyboy. Maybe wilder. Nobody in fifteenth-century Florence packed a six-shooter."

He chuckled and said, "Well, you ain't steered me wrong on my education yet, Miss Inga. But would it be fair to say you've been trying to educate me so much because schoolmarms find it almost as tough as lady docs to meet men worth knowing in the middle of a prairie?"

She lowered her lashes and turned a handsome shade of pink as she cut around him to go fetch the book she'd been talking about from the stacks. When she brought it back he stared at it dubiously. For though it was a thin book, it was printed in small type and he could see there were thunder-gastingly long words on the very first page. He sighed and said, "Well, I'll give her a go. You say this old boy knew his stuff?"

She'd recovered enough to reply calmly, "He lived through many a change in mighty changing times. Pay attention to the two-faced tricks the Borgia outfit went in for, Matt. What a man tells you, smiling, isn't always what he means to do when your back is wider open to him, see?"

Taylor grimaced and said, "I can't see why neither of you gals think much of poor old Big Bill. Even if he was out to do me dirt, he wouldn't have to trick me sneaky. He hired me to begin with and he could fire me this instant if he was the least annoyed with me."

She shrugged and replied, "He could if he spent that much time at his desk, or if he thought the town council would *let* him. I never said Marshal Burton was out to do you dirt, Matt. I simply think any man on the rise ought to read Machiavelli. It's only thanks to the U.S. Bill of Rights that *The Prince* can be sold on the open market today. King Henry VIII ordered every copy in Merry England burned, after only reading one. He felt it most unfair to give away trade secrets. Of course, he used more than a few of Machiavelli's suggestions, and his daughter, good Queen Bess, must have read the family copy."

Taylor put *The Prince* atop the other books he'd just checked out, saying, "I sure hope it gives some tips on gents who die in town, unmourned by even their pony. I've sure been scratching my head over that event. So far nobody's seen hide nor hair of at least four pals who used to ride in once a week with the poor fat cuss."

Then he left to tote the books to the lockup. He had to read 'em somewhere, and with folk asking pointed questions about the real boss, it seemed best to keep the office open at least until bedtime, lest someone want to report a pest and make even more pointed comments when they found no law at all on duty.

It was after four in the afternoon and looked later. For the sky above had clouded over and a light snow was starting to

drift down. The wind was still. If it didn't pick up, blowing
from the northwest or northeast, there wouldn't be enough
snow to fret about, come morning. But he hoped Tim
Hogan had thought to split some extra stove-wood. Tim
wasn't good for much else, and it was getting sort of nippy.

As he approached the lockup he saw three bay ponies
tethered out front and picked up his pace. The brown rumps
steamed where snowflakes landed. The stock looked as if it
had been ridden some already. He went on inside to find the
brownnosing Tim had already poured coffee for the three
visitors. They stared at him curiously. He saw one was a
white man with a handlebar mustache and eyes that looked
right through one. The other two were smooth-shaven
Indians or breeds. All three of them wore federal badges on
their sheepskin jackets. Taylor put the books aside and
introduced himself. The white lawman, who seemed to be
in command, shook firmly and announced, "I'd be Deputy
U.S. Marshal William Tilghman from the Indian Nation.
I'd like you to meet Officers Tallchief and Yellowpony of
the Osage Police."

Taylor shook with the Indians as well. Tallchief was sort
of hatchet-faced, and Yellowpony was more moon-faced.
Otherwise they both looked as much alike and about as
friendly as a pair of wooden warriors carved for the tobacco
trade. Taylor accepted the mug Tim Hogan handed him and
told the tall white federal lawman, "It's a real honor to meet
you, sir. I've heard a lot about you. Your pal, Charly
Siringo, passed through here just a spell back. What can I
do for you boys?"

Tilghman said, "We got the all-points you sent out. We
found it mighty interesting. The dead man you described
answers to what we know about a habitual cow thief best
knowed as Fats Gordon. He was last seen riding north with
a herd of cows trail-branded 808. Siringo had already wired
us, from Nebraska, that him and his sidekick, Rogers, had

rounded up some of the crooks already. But that others, including two ringleaders, had escaped."

Taylor whistled and said, "I can say for a fact that the fat one came through with the herd that time. But when Siringo come through, he said he was searching for government beef, not no 808 outfit."

Tilghman nodded curtly and said, "Steal me a cow branded US and then run its brand for me, son."

Taylor pictured such a brand, tried to decide how it could best be run, and then he gasped and said, "Oh Lord, you sure must think I'm dumb. For as soon as you study on it you can see how easy it would be, working backwards, to change an S to an eight, the U to an 0, and just add one extra eight!"

Tilghman nodded grimly and said, "You had an excuse. Nobody'd told you to watch for a run US. Charly Siringo's been at the job longer." Then the old pro sipped more coffee, lowered the cup again, and said, "We figure the ringleaders, along with the late Fats Gordon, knew better than to ride on south through the Indian Nation, knowing they'd been exposed and that many a hungry Indian was sore as hell about it. We figure they holed up around Freewater, knowing it's sort of out of the way once it gets too crisp for heavy traffic on the Ogallala Trail. You know this country. We don't. So the next move is up to you, Matt."

Taylor told Tim Hogan to run down to the livery and fetch him a mount. As the eager-to-please crawfisher left on the double, Taylor turned back to the federal lawmen to say, "It's a long shot. But I've been wondering about the riders who run off and left a pal to die alone in a whorehouse. Neither them nor their mounts could be in town. It ain't that big a town. There's only one spread on the surrounding prairie that would be close enough for them to ride in once a week the way they was doing until the way Fats died likely spooked 'em into lying lower for a spell. All but one of the soddies close enough to matter are *occupied*. Of course, if they're hiding out with crooked locals, all bets are off."

Tilghman nodded but said, "Let's start with the deserted place you just mentioned, then." To which Taylor replied, "It ain't deserted total. The woman and kids who own it are staying in town right now. Her man run off after giving her a beating, see?"

Tilghman grimaced and insisted, "Why the place was left to stand empty ain't near as serious as whether anyone's there *now*. How far a ride are we talking, with night coming on and snow coming down as well?"

Taylor said, "The Hatfield soddy's less than three full miles out to the northeast. The door and windows face due south, of course. The side and back walls are blank, last time I looked. They might have punched loopholes through the sod by now. On the other hand, they were likely camped in a draw until the last cold spell. There's a sort of overlap betwixt the first time they rode in to get laid and the more recent time the Hatfield house would have been theirs for the taking. So I could well be leading you boys on a snipe hunt."

Tilghman shrugged and said, "We got to start somewheres."

The four of them rode out under a darkening sky of wet wool with snowflakes trying to sneak in under their hat brims to sting their faces. They'd already agreed their best approach would be a wide swing around to ride into the Hatfield homestead from the hopefully blind side. That gave Matt Taylor time to observe to Tilghman, "I could see as you was buttoning up your sheepskin that you must have sawn off a foot of your Buntline Special, Marshal Tilghman. That's what I'd do if I'd been given one, I reckon. A pistol with a rifle barrel must be a bitch to draw, right?"

The federal lawman growled, "Call me Bill. I'm only a deputy marshal, anyway. As to my sidearm, it's a plain old Colt .44–40, like most gents carry. It takes the same shells as my saddle gun, and there are times a man don't want to get confused when he's reloading under fire. Who told you that fool tale of Buntline's foolish whatevers? I've heard the gossip before, and I've been wondering who started it."

Taylor frowned thoughtfully and replied, "I thought I got it from the horse's mouth. Weren't you at the Long Branch in Dodge, along with Bat Masterson, Wyatt Earp, Big Bill Burton, and some other famous lawmen when Ned Buntline presented you all with the guns he had made up special in your honor?"

Tilghman chuckled and replied, "I've spent many an evening in the Long Branch. I was the marshal there, a spell. I never met the late Ned Buntline. Read some of his foolish stories about Buffalo Bill and poor old James Butler Hickok, though. Lord knows where old Ned got such wild notions for his Wild West magazines. When was this great event supposed to have taken place?"

Taylor said, "The summer of 1876, no?"

So this time Tilghman really laughed before he said, "I'd have been in Dodge about then as a green kid younger than you could be right now. The Masterson boys, Ed and Bat, might have been there as early as seventy-six, but they wouldn't have been well known that early. As for Wyatt Earp, his elder brother, Virgil, was as noted a lawman as that family ever produced. I think young Wyatt had been arrested as a horse thief in the Indian Nation by seventy-five or seventy-six. I know Big Bill Burton as the marshal of Freewater, of course. Can't say I ever *met* him, early or late. You say these prize guns we was all supposed to get at the Long Branch in seventy-six have *rifle* barrels?"

Taylor nodded and said, "Carbine barrels, leastways. Big Bill still packs his, no matter where or when he got it.

Sixteen-inch barrel on a Model Seventy-six Peacemaker
frame. Are you sure you might not have been paying
attention that day in the Long Branch, Bill?''

Tilghman shook his head and said, ''I never drank *that*
much in Luke Short's joint. But hold on; I think I recall the
freaksome Colt you're jawing about. You still see it now
and again in old Colt catalogs. They tried to put that model
out in time for the Centennial of 1876. It never caught on.
The notion that a man had use for a weapon that was neither
a good rifle nor a decent six-shooter looked better on paper
than in a gun shop. Colt was stuck with the few they made
that year. Their Model Seventy-four still sells. This Model
Seventy-eight I'm packing is double action and even better.
You say your boss packs a single-action thumb buster with a
sixteen-inch barrel? Business must be mighty slow in these
parts, no offense.''

Matt Taylor didn't answer. He felt mighty sheepish as he
considered how Big Bill had greened him with tales of
wonder and a gun he'd likely picked up cheap in some hock
shop. It was small wonder Big Bill kept grinning down at
him and calling him his ''old son.'' Green hands were
always falling for tall tales about side-running mustangs and
hoop snakes. Big Bill had surely taken him in with that tale
of the Buntline Special. He'd told it so real, with a straight
face, the humorous cuss.

He reined in on a gentle rise to point southeast at a dark
blur just visible through the falling snow. As the others did
the same, he said, ''Yonder's the Hatfield homestead.
Nobody inside ought to know we're here, even if they've
loopholed. There'd be few reasons for anyone to be riding
in from this direction in a snowstorm.''

Yellowpony said, ''Heya, there is smoke rising.'' And as
if not to be outdone, Tallchief said, ''I see it. I see ponies,
too. I see five ponies in the corral, huddled together in the
wind shadow closer to the sod house.''

The two white men had to stare harder. Tilghman
chuckled and said, "I brung 'em along because Indians are
part eagle. One of them ponies would be the one Fats used
to ride. So that makes her four, at least, we got to deal
with."

As the U.S. deputy took the lead to drift in at a slow
walk, Tallchief grinned wolfishly and said, "Hear me. If
one of us moves in fast, leaps to the flat roof from his pony,
and puts his hat over the stovepipe, we can shoot the bad
men as they come out, smoked and blinded, no?"

Bill Tilghman shook his head and answered, "No. I
admire your notion about smoking them out. But folk can
get hurt, shooting wild in a smoky snowfall. It's always best
to use sweet reason, if you can."

As they moved in closer, with no sign from the house that
they might have been spotted, Tilghman reined in near the
two-strand fence the missing Hatfield had strung during a
lull in his wife beating and announced, "We'd best move in
the rest of the way afoot. Tallchief, seeing you're so
ambitious, what say you edge off to the east to chase their
ponies outten yon corral?"

Then they all drew their saddle guns, dismounted,
tethered, and moved forward, abreast but spread out right.
As Tallchief made for the corral, Tilghman led Taylor and
Yellowpony to the west wall of the soddy. It was blank, as
Taylor had promised. The federal lawman sighed and said,
"Some old boys are mighty dumb. Of course, if they was
smart, they'd make as much or more at an honest trade."

Taylor soon saw Tilghman had worked with the two
Indians before. On the far side, Tallchief timed things just
right. The white deputy marshal was in position at one
corner of the house, with his Winchester trained to rake the
whole south front, as the Indian policeman dropped the gate
poles to the frozen earth and sent the five ponies on their

way across the now white prairie with a couple of pistol
shots and a fiendish Osage war cry.

The front door popped open soon thereafter. Bill Tilghman put a bullet hole in it. So whoever had meant to come
out stayed put, the door still gaping, as the federal lawman
called out, almost pleasantly, "You boys in the house. I
hope I have your undivided attention. You are listening to
the words of U.S. Deputy Marshal William Tilghman, and
it's my sad duty to inform you that I'm ready to take you all
back to the Indian Nation now. So dress warm, toss your
guns out first, and we'll be on our way, hear?"

A hoarse voice called back, "Go to hell. We ain't ready
to go nowheres with nobody, you bastards!"

Tilghman's voice remained calm as he called back, "Sure
you are. We got you boxed in with no ponies, and snow-
covered prairie as far as the eye can see in any direction you
might want to try and outrun a rifle ball."

An arm in a checked sleeve reached gingerly out to try for
a grab at the door latch. Tilghman sent the hand back inside
and the door open wider with his second shot. As the sound
died away, he explained, "If we wanted it warmer inside,
we'd cap your stovepipe. Don't call me a bastard again. I
don't like it. You don't want to go all the way back to Fort
Reno with anyone who's mad at you, do you?"

There was a long silence. Then another, more pleading,
voice called back, "We can see the fix you got us in. We
know who you are as well, Mr. Tilghman. It's been said
you're sort of hard on gentlemen of the road you *ain't* all
that mad at. Who's to say the four of us would ever get to
Fort Reno alive if we did take you up on your kind offer?"

Tilghman said, "Me. I considers it the mark of a
professional to bring my wants in alive. Have you boys ever
heard of old Bill Doolin? You should have. Him and his
gang was a lot more famous than *you* piss ants."

The trapped cow thief replied sullenly, "We heard about the Doolin gang. What about 'em?"

Tilghman replied, "I took Bill Doolin, personal, alive, after he'd boasted no such thing would ever happen. I could have killed him. Some say I *should* have killed him. I didn't. He gave up like the smart gent he was when he saw I had the drop on him."

There was no answer. But Taylor could hear the buzz of heated discussion inside. Tilghman called out, "In eighty-four I had a chance to gun the Indian Nation's answer to Billy the Kid. But I shot a pony out from under the snarlsome kid instead. Had to spank the brat afore I got the cuffs on, too. But I figured it was well worth my effort once I discovered it was a teenage *gal* I'd run to earth. We called her Little Britches. My point is that Little Britches and her pal, Cattle Annie, wound up in reform school instead of dead. They'd likely both be out, reformed, by this time. You boys come along decent and you have my word you'll get a fair trial and no more'n ten or twenty years if you behave your fool selves. On the other hand, do you insist on turning this situation ugly, I can't say who I'll be taking back alive or dead, once we commence tossing dynamite down your stovepipe." He paused to let that sink in. Then he said, "You got three minutes to talk it over and make up your minds. It's cold out here, too."

It was more like thirty seconds before the first six-gun flew out the open door, followed in short order by three more and five rifles. Bill Tilghman chuckled and said, "That looks about right. Now we want you to come out single file, hands high, and just walk south till you hear me tell you to turn around."

They did. Tilghman halted the quartet of unwashed and unshaven cow thieves five yards out on open prairie before he had his Indian helpers handcuff and pat them down. As Tilghman and Matt Taylor strode to join them, their red-headed leader stared at them to demand, "Is this all of you there was? We thought you had a whole posse out here, Bill."

Tilghman smiled thinly and said, "I was bluffing about that dynamite as well. But a few good men are generally enough, when they know what they're doing. I fear we're going to have to walk you boys into town. But it ain't all that far, and you can always consider the happy thought that you're walking instead of having to be carried. Tallchief, why don't you go fetch the ponies for the rest of us?"

As the Indian jogged away to do so, Tilghman told Taylor, "I'd be much obliged if we could lodge these boys in your fine patent cells overnight, Matt. Does this snow let up, we'll start herding 'em south after sunrise."

Taylor said he'd be proud to lock the federal prisoners up for the night. One of them shot Tilghman a wary look and muttered, "I sure hope you was planning on finding *us* some ponies to ride all that way, Mr. Tilghman." And when the federal lawman just smiled back, thinly, another protested, "Hold on. You surely ain't cruel enough to *walk* us all the way back to Fort Reno, are you?"

Bill Tilghman asked, "Why not? The cows you boys stole down in the Indian Nation had to walk even farther, didn't they?"

By election day the November winds were blowing from the north with mighty sharp teeth. Matt Taylor found it easy enough to get over to the schoolhouse, wrapped in his sheepskins. Most of the townsmen made it there as well. But as he hung up his hat and jacket in the coal-smoke-scented warmth of the polling place, he failed to see many men dressed as cow as he was. Given the choice of candidates, he doubted *he'd* risk a long ride in this sort of weather just to choose between the semieducated but ambitious rascals who wanted to get at the public trough.

The ballot box for Freewater was set up on a trestle table with poll watchers from opposing sides sitting by to glare at one another as gents came in to cast votes and talk about the weather outside. Taylor found a corner seat and decided he could watch the box as well from there. Inga Larson came over to hand him a cup of coffee. As he took it with a nod of thanks, the willowsome blonde said, "You haven't been by the library since you and those men from the Indian Nation captured that gang of dangerous outlaws, Matt."

He smiled up at her to reply, "They wasn't as dangerous as old Bill Tilghman. I can see why he's so admired. I just tagged along for the ride. As to what I've been doing since, I've been trying to finish that book by Machiavelli in the spare time I've had. He sure uses big words. But you was right about him knowing how *sneaky* some folk act."

He saw she didn't seem to be moving away with her coffeepot. So he said, "There was a story about that Borgia rascal who set out to take over all the towns in them parts for his old dad, the pope. He figured it wouldn't look seemly, him being a prince of their church and all. So he had his sidekicks take this town, line up all the important folk there, and execute every one of 'em. Then old Borgia rode in to set himself up as the town law, and you know what he done then? He pretended to be surprised all the men who might have voted against him had been killed by his own men. He said they'd done it with no orders from *him*, had them all hung or worse, and everybody left *cheered* him as their sweet deliverer! He surely was a sly one, even for a furriner."

She nodded and said, "I was hoping you'd see things aren't always as honest as they seem. Who are you betting on to win this election today?"

He shot a casual glance over the crowd, shrugged, and decided, "Smiley and his bunch, most likely. I've seen more saloonkeepers than ministers so far."

As if to prove his point, Mayor Smiley came in, dropped his ballot in the box, and came over to join them. As Taylor rose to give the one seat to the pudgy banker, Smiley said, "No, thanks. I can't stay. Got to get to a council meeting. How come you never told us Bill Burton was running for a county seat, Matt?"

Taylor replied, "Nobody asked, and I thought you knew. He's been *saying* he'd like to be the new sheriff, openly enough."

Smiley scowled and snapped, "Running on the other party's ticket, wearing the badge we pinned on him, on day wages we've been paying him to work for *us*! We're going to have to send away for a marshal's badge for you, Matt. We'll be voting to fire the rascal at the meeting this afternoon. But he'll likely want to keep the badge we issued him. It's sort of tarnished in any case."

Taylor wasn't sure whether the mayor meant tarnished in the literal or figurative sense. He did know what he meant himself when he said, "I'll only be willing to take the promotion on more than one condition, sir. I'd want it in writing that it was the city council and nothing I might have done or said that cost Big Bill his job. Then, in writing or not, I'd want you and your council to back some changes I feel are needed."

Smiley said, "The first part's easy. We always send a notice of dismissal with the final paycheck. As to changes the council might or might not go along with, *you'd* best spell them out in writing as well."

Taylor nodded and said, "I mean to. It's too easy to say one thing and do another when there's no record on paper of who said what to whomever. But I reckon that can wait until we see who won this election, don't you reckon?"

Mayor Smiley smiled smugly and said, "It's in the bag. Save for a few prissy preachers who spend too much time sipping tea with our womenfolk, all the gents in town know which side their bread is buttered on."

He shot an awkward glance at Inga Larson as he added, "Until such time as the ladies get to vote—and praise the Lord and no offense, Miss Inga, it won't be in *my* time—the real world we all have to live in will be run by the men, who have to pay the tab and suffer the consequences. Female notions like the DAR and the WCTU cause enough trouble *without* the vote. Now I'd best run along to where the ways of this wicked world are *really* decided."

He must have known what he was talking about. For when the countywide votes were tallied over the next few days, all of the incumbents had won. Big Bill Burton's write-in campaign had not only failed, but had left him out of a job. Some said he was taking it mighty hard, with considerable drinking and downright ugly talk about the two-bit cowboy who'd stabbed him in the back and stolen his job as the marshal of Freewater.

By the time Matt Taylor had fired Tim Hogan, promoted Joe Walsh to senior deputy, and hired three roundsmen to patrol the streets around the clock on a regular basis, the sneaky climate of the High Plains had taken a turn for the better.

An unseasonable chinook from the west had burned off all the snow patches and even thawed the soil a mite. This was good for the native shortgrasses. They knew enough to lie doggo and stay straw stubble. Introduced weeds sprang up to take advantage of the warm spell. So the next cold snap was sure to nip most of them before they could set seed. The Indians had always held that Wakan Tonka had meant the High Plains to stay a rolling sea of grass that outside flora and fauna had to adapt to or die.

Hence Matt Taylor was wearing just his denim jacket over a heavyweight wool shirt the evening Freewater

Fannie sent Corks to ask the young new marshal if she might have a word with him.

Corks led him to the madam's larger business establishment rather than to her smaller and less bawdy private cottage. Taylor found the aging but still handsome redhead in a small office off the vestibule. She was seated at a rolltop desk in more ladylike wear than she'd had on the first time they'd met. She waved him to a window seat, finished an entry in her business ledger, and shut it to turn in her swivel chair to face him, staring at him with the unwinking gaze of a well-fed cat trying to make up its mind about a mouse.

He asked the old whore what he could do for her. She sighed and said, "You and your boys have been leaving me and my girls alone. That's more than we're accustomed to at the hands of trail-town lawmen. Do you know that since you took over, we haven't had to serve so much as a free drink in the parlor to anyone on your force?"

He shrugged and told her, "I've been trying to run things the way I figure professional lawmen like Bill Tilghman might. I'm pleased to hear my men have been behaving as decent as I told 'em to act. But surely that can't be what you wanted to talk to me about, Miss Fannie."

She shook her red mop and said, "No. it's important to what comes next, though. Bill Burton's back in town. He just left us after abusing two of my girls and one of my bottles past common decency. Marcel tells me he's up to the Prairie Dog right now, bragging on how he took you out of the gutter, gave you the only decent job you'd ever had, and so forth. Marcel thinks he'll be sending for you as soon as he's juiced up his courage enough."

Taylor sighed and said, "I was afraid he'd feel that way about the way he got fired through no fault of my own. I'd better get up there and calm him down before he burns any bridges ahint the two of us. It's harder to get out of an invite once it's been issued, and he'll likely calm down once he hears my side of it." *I Love you sweety*

Freewater Fannie said flatly, "He didn't ride in to have you calm him down, Matt. I told you he was *here* earlier. I sent for you because, before he left, he told me to. He's betting you won't be in fit shape for a fight after some time in my wicked clutches. You see, I've done such favors for him in the past. He seems to think I still owe him. Maybe I will, if he takes over this town again. How would you bet on that if you were me, good-looking?"

Taylor smiled thinly and replied, "There's nothing to bet on. Even if he killed me, the council would never give him his old job again."

She sniffed and told him, "You don't know those timid old he-goats as well as me and my girls, then. Town law is supposed to be able to take on all comers. They hired Bill Burton because of his size and his rep. They replaced him with you when you built a better rep. But he who wins is the one with the rep. It's as simple as that. So what happens next, handsome?"

He frowned thoughtfully and replied, "It sure seems simpler to establish a rep as a bronc peeler. Of course, both man and beast usually wind up alive after a bucking contest, no matter who wins. If I had a lick of sense, I'd just let him have his old job back and say no more about it."

She nodded and asked, "When do you mean to ride on, then?"

He said flatly, "I don't. There's sensible and there's *right*. It wouldn't be right to let this town be run by a man half as unprofessional as Big Bill, ungrateful as it may be. So I reckon I'll just have to go have a talk with Big Bill and see if I can get him to listen to reason."

She said, "You can't. He's already made up his mind to do you in dirty. I just told you he ordered me and the girls to set you up so's he can pluck you like a chicken. I thought it best to warn you instead. But by now Corks will have told him you came here as requested. He'll figure we set you up for him, as we've done others for him in the past. It won't put him in the mood for sweet reason. He knows he has to take you, and he knows—or let's say, he *thinks* he knows— he'll never have a better edge on you."

Taylor frowned at her warily and asked, "Just what have you ladies been doing to customers Big Bill might want to have hard words with later? I hope you understand that whilst unlicensed drinking and worse can be ignored, provided you keep it down to a roar, as well as in Kansas, I can't hardly overlook slipping odd stuff in a man's drink and sending him out of here too drugged to know what he might be aiming at."

She favored him with a sneaky little Mona Lisa smile and said, "You have my word I wouldn't do a thing like that. Let's just say there's more than one way to skin a cat, or Delilah a would-be Samson, and let it go at that until we see who wins."

He smiled thinly and got to his feet as he said, "The Good Book allows old Samson spent too much time in places like this for his own good, no offense. Maybe I can get Big Bill to tell me what this is all about. It's been nice talking to you, ma'am."

As he left, the old bawd called after him. "Have your own gun out when you stride into the Prairie Dog, honey. I'll never speak to you again if you get your fool self killed!"

He strode west in the gathering gloom, chuckling, until he asked himself what was so funny. As he crossed the Ogallala Trail and headed up Main Street, Joe Walsh fell in beside him, saying, "Big Bill's forted up in the Prairie Dog, making war talk that sounds serious, boss."

Taylor said, "I heard. You'd best wait over to the office, Joe. There seems to be some confusion about just who you'll be working for in the morning. You'd best stay out of it. I could lose."

Joe Walsh said stubbornly, "I don't want you to lose. You may need more backup than I can offer. That French-Canuck pimp as works for Freewater Fannie is seated at a corner table in the very same saloon."

Taylor insisted, "Go back to the office and find your own spot to sit. That's an order. I doubt Marcel cares half as much as me about the outcome. He'll be acting more like an interested observer. Him and his kind will be anxious to throw in with the winner, but not anxious to take a chance on siding with the loser."

They argued about it some more. But then Walsh peeled off to cross to the town lockup, muttering to himself. The saloon was an all-too-short farther, cuss its batwing entrance. Taylor did remember Freewater Fannie's warning. But he left his .44–40 in its holster just the same. He was out to prevent a war, not to start one, if that was still at all possible.

He could see as he entered that this hardly seemed possible. Big Bill Burton was down at the far end of the bar with his back to the wall and both a schooner of beer and the Buntline Special reposing on the mahogany within easy reach of the giant's right paw. This was easy enough to make out at a glance because not one other man was at the bar between them. The saloon was almost empty. Only Marcel and a few other wiseass onlookers were seated at a discreet distance, against the far wall from the bar.

As Taylor moved to close the gap between them, wearing as sincere a smile as he could manage, Big Bill snapped, "That's far enough, sonny. I was just fixing to send for you. We got some things to settle, you ungratesome stray pup."

Taylor said, "I heard. You got things all wrong, Big Bill. I never stole your job. You threw it away."

Big Bill shrugged and said, "Maybe I did. Maybe I

didn't. In either case, I want it back. So for old times' sake, I'm giving you a mighty generous choice. You can unpin that badge, put it on the bar, and ride out of town before midnight, or you can go for your gun. Your move, Matt."

Taylor took a deep breath, let half of it out so his voice wouldn't crack, and replied, "I don't take my orders from you anymore, Big Bill. It's not for you or me to say who wears the top badge in this town, and you know I don't want to gun anybody. I had the honor of riding with real lawmen a short time ago. I couldn't help noticing that professionals don't use their guns unless they really have to."

Big Bill said flatly, "You really have to. There's but one Lord in heaven, one sun in the sky, and one marshal of this town. I'm it." Then his big right paw was reaching for the Buntline Special on the bar.

Even as he went for his own gun, Taylor knew there was just no way he was going to beat Big Bill. Time seemed to slow down and his brain seemed to split in two as he hauled his own .44–40 out and up through air that seemed thicker than molasses. One part of him was pleading for its life and begging him to do something—anything to end this nightmare, while, at the same time, another part of him remained a detached observer, more bemused than frightened by events that just couldn't be happening. Then Big Bill had the Buntline Special trained at him, the barrel so long it seemed to go off at point-blank range, to punch Taylor's breastbone with a big fist. Then, even as part of him wondered how the rest of him was still functioning with a bullet in his heart, the six-gun in his own hand was aiming and firing as if it had a life of its own.

Big Bill's second shot tore Taylor's Stetson off. His third was aimed at the tin ceiling as the giant's more human-sized foe kept throwing lead his way through the now dense fog of black-powder smoke. Then Taylor's hammer clicked on an empty shell and he realized, sickly, that he'd spent all he had in the wheel.

But as he peered through the now-thinning smoke, he saw that Big Bill Burton had lowered the Buntline Special to his side as he stood there, blank-faced, leaning against the wall. Then his knees buckled and the huge man slid slowly down the wall until Taylor could see the cluster of bullet holes he'd punched through the paneling, and the streaks of blood Big Bill was painting with the back of his shirt as he slid all the way down and wound up reclining on the sawdust floor with his head pillowed on the brass rail of the bar.

As he moved closer gingerly, Taylor heard Marcel warning the other witnesses that while the young marshal's gun seemed to be empty, *his* wasn't. Taylor kicked the Buntline Special a safer distance from Big Bill before he hunkered down by the fallen giant to murmur, "Hey there, Big Bill?"

His former boss and mentor opened a pair of eyes that were already glazing to whimper in a little-boy voice, "Don't tell on me, pard. I just hate it when folk laugh at me. Don't you?"

Taylor began to reload as he asked the man he'd emptied his gun into what they might be talking about. Big Bill didn't answer. He couldn't. Taylor reached out with his free hand to close the glassy dead eyes. Then he rose to his feet again and felt the front of his own shirt. His chest felt bruised and his shirt front felt greasy. He couldn't see any blood on his fingertips when he held them up to the light. But there were tiny flecks of what certainly looked like untarnished lead.

He muttered, "What the hell?" and then the place began to fill with others who'd responded to the thunderous sounds of gunplay. Someone who'd been there answered the questions of a newcomer by shouting, "You just missed a shoot-out for the ages. The late Bill Burton was just dumb enough to try for the one and original Matt Taylor, with predictable results."

Taylor spotted Joe Walsh in the crowd and hailed his senior deputy over. When Walsh got a first good look at the monstrous cadaver in the corner, he gasped and said, "Jesus H. Christ, boss. Did you do that all by yourself?"

Taylor said, "I had to. Now I got to do something else. So I want you to take charge here, Joe. You know the moves to be made. I'll join you all later at the wagon wright's, Lord willing and the creeks don't rise."

Walsh nodded and said, "Sure, boss. Ain't nobody fixing to argue with *you* in this town for the foreseeable future!"

Taylor retrieved his hat and the Buntline Special from the sawdust. He brushed them both off and put the Stetson on his head and the still warm barrel of the clumsy weapon down the front of his jeans. He looked about for Marcel, failed to see him, and left with a shrug to retrace his earlier steps from the red-light district.

He found Freewater Fannie in her office, where it seemed he'd left her at least a year ago. The faded redhead already had a bottle and two glass tumblers ready on her rolltop. As she began to pour she said, "Marcel just told me. Sit down, handsome. This is an occasion to celebrate indeed."

Taylor chose the same window seat. But as she held out a drink to him, he shook his head and said, "Not hardly. Not until you tell me just how you Delilahed Big Bill and all those other would-be Samsons, ma'am."

The old bawd sighed and said, "I learned long before I was your age never to speak freely to the law without my lawyer there to hold my hand and keep my foot out of my mouth. Let's just say Bill Burton was here earlier, asking for the usual services, on the house. I was willing to let him have French Fifi and all he wanted to drink, gratis. But I thought he was pushing his luck when he told me to set you up for him the same way others had been set up in the past. I know what you think of me and mine, Matt. But I think you're a sweet young boy as well as one hell of a lawman."

Taylor shrugged modestly as he hauled the Buntline Special out of his jeans, saying, "So you figured it was in your own interest to set up Big Bill instead?"

She didn't answer. But she watched as Taylor began to unload the notorious gun-slick's cylinder. The three unspent rounds in the palm of his left hand looked fresh from the box and not at all unusual. He raised one to his face and bit into the silvery slug. Then he grimaced, spat the chewed-up bits of wax back in his palm, and said, "When I was in school they let us draw with gold and silver crayons. Even if a poor sap checked his gun as he left here, these wax slugs would likely lull him into a false sense of security."

Freewater Fannie sighed and said, "It was never my notion, nor the notion of anyone working for me, Marshal honey. Bill Burton cast them almost harmless bullets in all calibers and issued 'em to us his own self, see?"

Taylor did. He nodded and said, "Growing up so big and tough-looking likely failed to provide him with as much practice at fighting as most men get, whether they want it or not. Nobody bullies the bully of the school or town, as a rule. He must have felt he needed an edge on those few who *were* brave enough to take him on. A man would have to be *loco*, or good, to stand up to a gent who looked like the Cardiff Giant had escaped from Barnum. The big old gun he found in some hock shop helped him some. It was a modest way to brag on being a famous gunfighter all the way back to seventy-six. But when nothing else seemed to work, he got you and your gals to reload for wilder men working themselves up for a showdown the usual way, right?"

She blushed under her face paint as she told him, "We were supposed to outfit you with wax .44–40s while you were calling on me earlier this evening. I sent word to him I had, by entertaining you personal. I hope you ain't too insulted. I did it to spite him at you even more. You see, despite his brag around town, that's the one thing I never gave him. I figured the other nice things we had to do to stay on the good side of the law was more than enough.''

Taylor smiled thinly and said, "You sure had him too sore at me to consider checking his own gun as he waited to thump me as hard as I ever want to be thumped with a wax bullet. I can't say I'm entirely displeasured with the results of your prank this evening. He had me, had that been a real bullet he aimed at my poor heart. For he was good as well as yellow-streaked. How come you never told me about wax bullets, even after I wound up the top town law, Miss Fannie?''

She asked simply, "Would you have faced off with Bill Burton tonight, knowing his famous gun couldn't do you any real harm?''

He thought, gulped, and decided, "I'll have doubtless felt honor-bound to warn him and give him the choice of reloading or leaving town polite.''

She said, "I know. Marcel and I talked about that. The brute would have laughed it off as a joke on both of you. Then he'd have waited for a chance to back-shoot you. So all in all, we felt some secrets were best kept from the children until they were a mite older.''

He took another pull on her corn squeezings. It didn't help. He said, "To tell the truth, I feel more foolish than older. I've been taking credit for the Redford brothers, and now Big Bill, when all the time it was dirty tricks!''

She snapped, "Don't talk like a penny-dreadful hero. They were at another house. We couldn't get at their guns. You did nail all three of them as fairly as they'd have nailed you, and if you ever say one word about having any edge on anyone, we'll have every gun-happy yahoo west of the Big Muddy coming here to try their luck with you and all our window glass. So be a good boy and let sleeping dogs lie. You're supposed to be a peace officer, not a one-man war, damn it.''

He repressed a shudder as her words sank in. He nodded and said, "Old Bill Tilghman would have had a lot more trouble with them cow thieves if even one of 'em had him down as a four-flusher. I reckon it would be more professional to take your advice and just go along with being a sort of legend. Everyone I've shot so far seems to have been half-bull."

She'd finished her glass and asked if he'd like another as she served herself. He shook his head and said, "I dasn't even finish this one. I got some tedious chores ahead of me when I leave here. I don't want it said the famous Marshal Taylor needs to get likkered up every time he guns a cuss. But seeing as you give such good advice on the way folks think, Miss Fannie, I got more personal things than gunfighting on my mayhaps immature mind. You see, I've met these two ladies since I've been here in Freewater, and they've got me all mixed up about the Thanksgiving dance they'll be holding at the Grange Hall any time now."

She said bluntly, "Go with the one you like best. You'll never get rid of free stuff you take to any fool dance, you know."

He nodded and said, "I know nobody but a Mormon is allowed to spark two gals at once. That's what's got me so mixed up. You see, I ain't good enough for either of 'em and I'd be lucky to wind up with either. I just don't know which one I ought to be the *most* in love with. One's a good kisser who's shown she's ready to fight for me with a gun. The other ain't as excitable, but she's just as pretty and I owe *her* a lot, too."

Freewater Fannie shot him an arch look and said, "When a man or a woman can't make up his or her mind about two possible loves, he or she ain't in love with either. I fell in love one time. In my case once was more than enough. So take it from one who's been there. If you ain't so sure that it *hurts*, you ain't in love with *nobody*!"

She leaned back in her chair, sensually, to add, "If you're just hard up, why go to strangers? I'd sure like to take such a nice young boy home to raise."

He laughed weakly and said, "Don't tempt me. You could be right. For I have to admit I've been having dirty thoughts in bed about both the ladies in question. I sure would like to get one or the other out of her duds long enough to see if I've guessed right."

Freewater Fannie sighed and said, "I'd like to see *you* in that condition, too. But since you seem to feel I'm your kindly old aunt or something, damn it, I can only point out that no matter *which* of them more prim and proper brats you pick, you're likely to always wonder what you missed by not choosing the *other* one. It's hard as hell to remain content with a wife you're *really* in love with, Matt. In my business you learn things like that about menfolk. So if I was you, I'd wait a spell afore I got settled down entire. You're young, good-looking, and just now starting to rise in the world. Why don't you hold your fire until you see a target worth shooting for?"

He shrugged and said, "You don't know how swell both the gals I'm discussing really are." To which she replied, "The hell you say. I hear all the gossip in this town. It's no secret you have both Helen Harris and Inga Larsen goofy over you. They'll both be at that dance, whether you take one or not. Why don't you just show up alone so's you can dance with *both* of 'em, and all the *other* young gals there, you fool kid?"

He grinned and rose to his feet, saying, "Well, maybe it is a mite early to post the banns with any old gal. I sure thank you for such motherly advice, Miss Fannie. My real ma died afore I got old enough to talk dirty with her."

She said, "Oh, get out of here afore you wind up arresting me for child molesting." So they parted friendly.

Outside, the sky was clear and the Milky Way seemed to

hang so low a man could scoop stars from it with his hat if he stretched a mite. The night air was brisk but dry and not all that cold, with the prairie wind holding its breath for now. He felt a lot better walking back to the center of town than he'd felt the last time he'd done so that same evening. When he got across from the town lockup he saw Joe Walsh lounging in the open doorway. So he cut across to ask how come his senior deputy didn't seem to be waiting at the wagon wright's, as he'd been told. Joe Walsh said, "We got Big Bill over there. It wasn't easy. They're making him a box. Looks like it's meant to ship a sofa somewheres. I tried to get Doc Crane to meet you there. But he said it could wait until morning in this weather. He's entertaining company from back east. I just met 'em. The head of the family is a dentist Doc Crane met up with during the war, when they was both serving in the Union army. He says he might set up a practice out here. His wife seems a nice lady, albeit on the snooty side, and as for their daughter, watch out! She looks like one of them Gibson gals stepped smack outten a magazine. With all due respect to my Lucy, gals like that make many a married man wish he'd waited. For if I was single, I know who *I'd* be taking to the Thanksgiving dance at the Grange Hall, and likely for a Christmas sleigh ride as well, if she'd go."

Taylor stepped inside to lay the Buntline Special on the desk as he said, "Well, a dentist should make out well during cattle drives. You say they seem sort of quality, Joe?"

Walsh nodded and said, "I don't think Doc Crane wants them knowing he treats wicked ladies over to the east end. Doc had a fresh shirt on and he acted mighty prim when he introduced me all around. If they stay long enough to matter, they may wind up reforming the old quack. The young gal said she's never been to a coroner's hearing and asked all about you. I told her you was a famous lawman. I didn't think you'd mind. How come you're throwing them pistol rounds in the stove, boss? Ain't they likely to go off?"

Taylor said, "The brass looked corroded. I doubt they'll do serious damage. I seem to have sort of inherited this foolish Buntline Special. I don't know whether to saw a foot off the barrel so's we might get some use out of it or just hang it on the wall as a sort of relic, seeing it's supposed to be some sort of prize."

Joe Walsh said, "It's your'n to do with as you like. You'd better let me introduce you to that new gal in town afore that dance, boss. She's sure to have her dance card filled, total, as soon as the other gents see what's come to town."

Taylor said he'd study on it overnight. Walsh smiled at him wistfully and said, "Suit yourself, you carefree cuss. I wish *I* was in position to treat good-looking gals as casual. How come a healthy young gent with such a good job is still running free to pick and choose? I was younger than you are right now when my Lucy roped and branded me."

Taylor chuckled and said, "Careful planning, Joe. I figure it won't kill me if I keep my mouth shut and my eyes open just a mite longer."

Lou Cameron is a New York City author who created the "bible" for the popular LONGARM western series. In 1976 he won the Spur Award for THE SPIRIT HORSES. Cameron is also a writer of crime novels.

His latest western for Fawcett was THE GRASS OF GOODNIGHT.